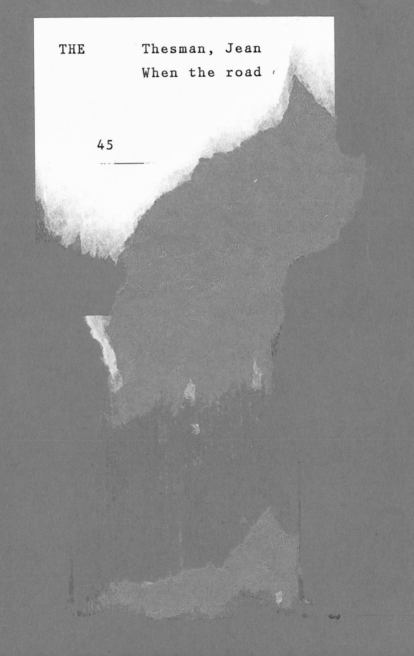

When the Road Ends

When the Road Ends

Jean Thesman

Houghton Mifflin Company
Boston

Library of Congress Cataloging-in-Publication Data

Thesman, Jean.
  When the road ends / by Jean Thesman.
    p. cm.
  Summary: Sent to spend the summer in the country, three foster
children and an older woman recovering from a serious accident are
abandoned by their slovenly caretaker and must try to survive on
their own.
  ISBN 0-395-59507-X
  [1. Foster home care—Fiction. 2. Physically handicapped—
Fiction. 3. Handicapped—Fiction. 4. Survival—Fiction.
5. Interpersonal relations—Fiction.] I. Title.
PZ7.T3525Wh 1992   91-14950
[Fic]—dc20   CIP
                         AC

Printed in the United States of America

BP   10 9 8 7 6 5 4 3 2

For Francine and Emily

When the Road Ends

◆ CHAPTER 1 ◆

In the winter when I was twelve, Adam Correy came to stay in the Percys' house with Jane and me. He was fourteen, and he had never lived with a foster family before. I could see that he'd decided he wouldn't like it.

"This isn't a bad place," I told him that first rainy afternoon when we were alone in his second-floor room.

He tossed his head, flipping back his straight blond hair so that he could stare at me. But he didn't say anything. After a long moment, he turned away and pulled clothes from the plastic bag he'd used as a suitcase.

"This is yours," I said, pointing to the small chest of drawers that Father Matt had painted tan, like the walls.

Adam shot another look at me, over his shoulder. "I know that," he said. "It's *my* bedroom."

My mouth had gone dry. "I was only making conversation."

"Well, quit it," he said. He stuffed his clothes into the top drawer and banged it shut.

"Father Matt will get you more clothes," I said. "He tries to help. If you need anything right away . . ."

"Do I have to go to confession first?" Adam asked.

"No!" I said. "He's Episcopalian, not Catholic. Didn't Mrs. Frank tell you that?" Mrs. Frank was the social worker who sent Adam, Jane, and me to live with Father Matthew Percy and his wife. Before I moved in, she had told me all about Father Matt, and I was sure she would have done the same for Adam.

Adam's stare unnerved me. I glanced away so I wouldn't see his light blue eyes glinting with an anger that burned cold instead of hot. "What did the priest say your name was?" he demanded.

"Mary Jack Jordan," I said.

"Is the little girl who lives here your sister?" he asked.

"Jane? No. She came a few months ago."

"What's wrong with her?" Adam asked. He was looking out the window now, watching the rain falling on the street below us.

When Father Matt brought Adam home to the rectory that Saturday afternoon, Jane had rushed upstairs and crawled under her bed. As usual, she hadn't uttered a sound.

"She doesn't talk," I said. "But she can hear."

"Is she retarded?"

I pulled Jane's latest drawing out of my pocket and unfolded it. "If she was retarded, she couldn't draw like this."

That morning, Jane had drawn the rectory with three figures beside it. One, a man, wore what looked like a necklace, and that probably was Father Matt's clerical collar.

Next to the man she'd drawn a figure that I knew was me, but don't ask me how. Except for the brown hair and blue eyes, it could have been anybody.

Next to me, Jane had drawn a skinny woman with her hair standing on end, and I had trouble not laughing when I saw it. I knew it was Mrs. Percy. Even if her hair didn't stand on end, she always acted as if it could, any minute. Father Matt said she was high-strung. All I knew was that she didn't have a sense of humor. Once I had called her "Mother Jill" just for fun, and she told me that I was never, ever to call her anything but Mrs. Percy.

This wasn't the best drawing in the entire world, but Jane was only seven or maybe eight years old. Nobody knew exactly, and since she didn't talk, no one could ask. In fact, no one knew her real name. Father Matt said that the social workers named her Jane

Smith so that they'd have something to write in their records.

There was no little figure representing Jane. There never was, not in any of her drawings.

Adam handed the paper back. "How long have you been here?" he asked. He sat on his bed, scowling, waiting for my answer.

Perhaps it was his expression that caused me to babble. Maybe I wanted to please him or explain myself. Anyway, I told him more than anybody had ever wanted to know about me.

"I don't remember my first foster family," I said, "the one that took me in after I was born. But I remember a little about the second family, Zuna and Bert. I moved away from them when I was three." And I still had the doll they gave me, too. But Adam wouldn't care about that.

"I liked the third family, the Nickersons, best," I went on. "But Ben had a stroke and Cally's arthritis got worse, so they couldn't keep me. I moved when I was seven." But Cally wrote me every week for a long time, I recalled, and I saved all the letters.

"Then came Gerta and Claude Bellows," I said. "They got a divorce after Christmas when I was eight." They had explained that it wasn't my fault. I hadn't liked them much anyway, especially after they got rid of their dog because he barked.

"When I was nine," I told Adam, "I moved in with the Petersons, and I stayed there until I was nearly twelve. They had to move to Nebraska because their folks needed them." I'd promised myself that I'd stop biting my fingernails if I could have my own family, but they never talked about adopting me.

"So," I concluded, "I've been here since last fall."

Adam blinked. I expected him to share his own story, even though Father Matt had already told me that Adam's mother had run off and left him alone. But he didn't say one single word. He watched me for a moment and then looked away, as if he'd suddenly seen something that caused him embarrassment.

A small, hot bubble of anger burst inside me. Furious with myself for talking too much, I stomped toward the door.

"Dinner's at six," I said. "If you get hungry before then, fix a sandwich. Don't go in the kitchen when Mrs. Percy is there, because it makes her nervous. You can watch television —"

"The priest told me," Adam said. He shook a paperback book out of his trash bag and lay back on the bed. "Get out," he added.

I went, and without slamming the door, either.

In the room I shared with Jane, she was still under her bed. I could leave her there until she came out on her own, which might not be for hours. Or I could coax her out and talk for a while.

I knelt beside her bed and peered under it. I could see her, scrunched all the way against the wall, sucking her thumb.

5

"I hope you didn't wet your pants again," I said. "If you did, will you come out now so I can clean you up?"

She didn't move.

"How about coming out to keep me company?" I said. "I'm not sure I like that boy very much. What do you think?"

She stayed against the wall, but one foot twitched a little, as if she wanted to say a number of things about that boy.

"Shall I read to you out of the animal book?" I asked.

Jane scrambled out, her dark eyes glowing. Lint was caught in her fine, pale hair. I took the brush off her shelf and tidied her up. "Nobody ever needs to dust under your bed," I said. "You keep it clean with your hair."

Jane didn't smile. I knew by her eyes that she heard me.

I opened the book to the page that told about baby bears, and we sat on the floor while I read. Rain pattered on the window. Jane sucked her thumb. The rectory was quiet.

Suddenly, downstairs, a door slammed. Something hit the old wood floor and bounced. Another door slammed. Mrs. Percy. Practically everything made her nervous. When she was nervous, she slammed doors — and anything else that was slammable.

My own door opened. Adam stood there, scowling. "What's going on down there?" he demanded.

"It's okay," I said. "It's just Mrs. Percy. She does that."

But Jane had frozen against me when she heard the first slam. Now, with Adam in our doorway, she was stiff with fright.

I slipped my arm around her, but it was too late. Crablike, she scuttled sideways under her bed.

"Jeez, what's wrong with her?" Adam asked. "She acts like somebody set fire to her."

A lump settled in my stomach. "Maybe somebody did," I said.

Adam stared me down. "Don't tell me about it," he said, and he left, closing the door firmly behind him.

Oh, thanks, I thought. That's all I need. One more person I can't talk to.

At dinner time, Mrs. Percy served tasteless chicken and gummy herb rice. Adam ignored the chicken and rice, but ate his canned corn and several pieces of bread. Jane ate next to nothing, but she seldom seemed hungry.

"You have to eat what's on your plate, because I won't fix you anything else," Mrs. Percy told Adam. "I came home exhausted, and I can see I went to all this trouble for another picky eater!"

She hadn't touched anything but her salad, and

Adam stared knowingly at her plate. "And *I* can see *you're* sticking to the stuff that can't kill you," he said.

Mrs. Percy covered her mouth with her napkin and left the table. Moments later I heard her bedroom door slam.

Father Matt cleared his throat, said, "Now, now," and then bent over his plate and chewed another bite of chicken. After that he tried hard to make it a cheerful meal, and I felt sorry for him. He had the same problem I had — talking too much. I was the only one who answered his questions, for Adam and Jane were pretending that he wasn't there. His thin face was flushed and his dark hair needed combing. He'd gotten a smudge of dirt on his collar. Sometimes I thought he needed to be taken care of more than I did.

Jane finished her milk and slid from her chair, scurrying toward the stairs. We ate our dessert in miserable silence.

Afterward, when Adam and I sat in the living room, he said, "Does the food ever get better?"

I looked up from the *TV Guide*. "It's usually pretty good," I said, "because Father Matt does most of the cooking. Mrs. Percy is always too tired. She's a teacher — I guess you know that — and kids make her nervous."

"Then why does she take in foster children?" Adam asked.

"It's Father Matt who really wants them — us," I said.

"We're his favorite charity, you mean?" Adam asked, angrier now than he was before.

I shrugged, uncomfortable with the conversation. "It has something to do with loving God," I said. "And loving thy neighbor and all that. He talks about it in church on Sundays."

"I don't go to church," Adam said.

"That's okay," I said. "Jane doesn't, either. Most of the time Mrs. Percy stays home on Sunday, too. After church, Father Matt takes us somewhere so we don't disturb her."

"Maybe *she'd* better not disturb *me*," Adam said, and he pulled his book out of his pocket and went to his room.

But Mrs. Percy disturbed Adam a lot over the next months.

"I can't stand how she jitters around," he complained one afternoon. "I hate people who slam doors and whine and complain."

"Noise bothers her," I said. "You turn up the TV so loud that her head aches. You don't wipe your feet when you come in the door. You're snotty to her. And you make trouble in school."

"How do you know what I do at my school!" he cried, outraged. "You're still in grade school."

"My friend Crystal has a brother in middle school, and he says you'll be suspended if you get into another fight."

I knew that Adam couldn't last. I'd been in homes before where one of the kids was dragged off by a social worker because he did stupid things. It was only because of what happened to Father Matt's sister that Adam wasn't thrown out. The Percys were too distracted by the tragedy to deal with him.

I barely knew Father Matt's sister, Cecile Bradshaw, even though she lived in Seattle. She and her husband had visited us briefly at Christmas, and Mrs. Percy got a terrible headache right away and had to lie down with a cold cloth on her head. It didn't take much to figure out that the women didn't like each other.

Then Mrs. Bradshaw was injured in a terrible car accident that killed her husband. She was in the hospital for weeks, all through the long, wet spring. A few days after she got out, Father Matt brought her home for dinner.

She'd had a head injury in the accident, and her concussion hadn't healed up yet. "But it will," Father Matt had told us before he picked her up. "Sometimes it takes a long time, maybe months, so you must be patient with her. And please, children, don't stare at the scar on her forehead."

"She should have worn her seat belt," Adam said.

"She did," Father Matt said. "That's why she's alive."

Mrs. Bradshaw was tall, like Father Matt, but her long brown hair was shot with gray, and one side of her face seemed twisted, almost like Ben's after he had his stroke. Father Matt had warned us about this. It, too, was because of the bad concussion.

But worst of all was Mrs. Bradshaw's speech. She hardly ever said anything throughout the long meal, but when she did, sometimes it didn't make much sense.

For instance, I asked her if she wanted butter for her bread. Instead of yes or no, she smiled crookedly, said, "Bread box thanks," and then burst into tears and left the table.

I was horrified. What had I done?

"It's all right," Father Matt had said quickly. "She still has a little aphasia. It embarrasses her."

"What's aphasia?" Adam asked.

"It means she has trouble with words," Father Matt said.

"It means she has *brain damage,*" Mrs. Percy said. "I told you not to bring her here, Matt. Now look what she's done. She's upset the children. I *told* you, but you never listen."

She was warming up to one of her fits again, and Father Matt tried to head her off. "They understand," he began.

11

"Sure," I said. "We aren't upset, are we, Adam?"

Adam, seeing an opportunity to annoy Mrs. Percy, said, "She's nice. And not half as crazy as some people around here."

Mrs. Bradshaw wouldn't come back to the table, and Mrs. Percy stumbled upstairs to her room with another cold cloth for her head.

"Maybe the priest will bring home somebody in a straitjacket tomorrow," Adam said, smirking, when we were alone.

"Shut up," I said. "That's mean."

"Did you see him cutting her meat for her?"

"It's because her left arm was injured," I said.

"You'd like anybody," he said, getting up from his chair.

Except you, I thought, wishing fiercely that he'd never moved in, because the trouble he caused might spill over on Jane and me.

Father Matt took his sister back to her apartment, where she lived alone now, and I wondered how she would manage, with only one good arm and not being able to speak clearly. Father Matt had told us that she couldn't see very well, either.

"Is it all right for Mrs. Bradshaw to live by herself?" I asked Mrs. Percy later, when she came to the kitchen for a glass of water. She needed it to wash down her nerve pills, she'd said.

"Of course it isn't all right," Mrs. Percy said. "She ought to be in an institution."

"But she'll be well again someday," I protested.

"All I know is that she isn't coming here," Mrs. Percy said, slamming the cupboard door. "I've got enough of a load."

Then, one evening in May while I was giving Jane her bath, I learned something that should have warned me that hard times were coming.

I'd been talking to Jane about barnyard animals while I soaped her back cautiously, barely touching the scar that ran across her shoulder blades. It was half as thick as my little finger — the biggest and ugliest of all the scars. Nobody knew how she got them, but Father Matt said that when she was found beside the freeway, she'd had raw, infected cuts on her back, and the doctors at the hospital thought that she'd been whipped with a chain. The scars on her neck were burns.

I'd just reached the part of my bath-time story about how milk comes from cows when Adam threw open the bathroom door and said, "That woman is coming here to live with us."

"Hey!" I cried. Jane had grabbed me so hard that she nearly pulled me in the tub with her. "Darn you, Adam. You know you aren't supposed to open the bathroom door when someone's in here."

"Did you hear me? That woman is moving in."

"What woman?" I asked as I pried Jane's arms loose.

"The priest's sister."

"But she can't," I said. "Mrs. Percy won't let her."

Adam jerked his head toward the stairs. "They're arguing about it now. The landlady where Mrs. Bradshaw lives called and said that she can't stay by herself because she forgets to eat. So the priest is bringing her here tonight and giving her my room."

I tried to judge from his eyes whether he was angry because he had to give up his bed or angry about something else.

"Maybe it won't be for long," I said, to soothe him so he'd shut the door and Jane wouldn't be in a panic any longer.

"It's bad enough being in the house with one crazy woman," Adam said. "I can't take two of them. I'll leave."

"Go ahead," I said, sighing. "Who cares?"

I meant it. I couldn't have guessed that before the week was over, Adam wasn't the only one who'd be leaving.

But when I remember that day, I think Jane must have had a premonition, because she looked up at me, wide-eyed with fright.

"It's okay," I said, even as I heard a door slam downstairs. "I'll take care of you."

I was right about that.

CHAPTER 2

Father Matt stayed home from his church office in the mornings to take care of Jane, because he couldn't afford a full-time baby sitter and she couldn't go to school. He left at noon, and horrible, fat Gerry Michaels arrived then. I knew she didn't help Jane, because Jane was always under her bed when I came home from school at three-fifteen. Under the bed and wet.

Each day Gerry took her fat scowl home exactly one minute after I returned. She could slam a door as well as Mrs. Percy. I don't know why she accepted the job of caring for Jane, since she loathed children — especially Jane — and, as she explained to me often enough, she could get any job she wanted, anytime.

"But I don't need a full-time job because my husband makes plenty of money," she told me.

I wished she would take one of those other jobs. She scared Jane, and she was lazy, so I ended up doing most of the housework.

On the day after we learned that Father Matt's sister was coming, Gerry told me that Jane's pants had been wet since noon, she'd refused to come out from under the bed even for lunch, and our social worker had called to say that she was coming at four to have a little visit.

Slam went the door behind Gerry. My stomach turned over painfully, and I rushed upstairs to the bedroom.

"Jane, get out of there," I cried as I threw myself down beside her bed. "Mrs. Frank is coming!"

Jane scrambled out. Maybe she didn't understand that Mrs. Frank could take us kids away and put us in other foster homes if she didn't like what she saw here. But Jane read my tone of voice. She ran for the bathroom while I found fresh clothes for her.

While I cleaned her up, I explained that things might go better if she'd talk. "And," I added, "don't run off and hide under the bed. No matter how scared you get, wait until Mrs. Frank is gone, okay?"

Jane's black eyes met mine. I knew she agreed to act brave, but talking was too much to expect.

I heard the kitchen door open and close downstairs. Adam. He'd have to be warned. He danced on the edge of disaster during Mrs. Frank's inspections. But now it was important that he behave.

There was another problem, too. The house would be crowded after Cecile Bradshaw arrived. Social workers didn't like crowded houses. Jane and I should

16

have had separate bedrooms, and the den should have been turned into a room for Adam. The possibilities for disaster scared me. I didn't want to move again.

I left Jane sitting on her bed with the animal book and ran downstairs.

"Mrs. Frank is coming," I babbled to Adam. "Don't do anything stupid or you'll end up somewhere awful."

"Worse than this bughouse?" he said, scornful and arrogant.

"Believe me, there are worse places," I said. "Quick, hang up your jacket and wash your hands."

He tossed his jacket over the back of a kitchen chair and opened the refrigerator. I sighed, giving up, and ran to the phone. I had memorized the number at the church office.

Father Matt's secretary answered, and when I told her who was calling, she said, "Father's busy, Mary Jack. Can't it wait until he gets home?"

"No," I said. "Tell him Mrs. Frank is coming. Please! Be sure to tell him. She's coming at four."

Father Matt must have flown the two blocks home, because I'd hardly reached my bedroom when I heard his shouted "Hello everybody!" in the kitchen and the sound of him taking the stairs two at a time.

"Well, well," he said from our doorway. He rubbed his hands together. His thin face was flushed. "Here are my girls, all dressed up for our friend."

"Are you going to tell Mrs. Frank about your sister?" I asked, afraid of his answer no matter what it would be.

He stopped rubbing his hands. "Cecile will only be here a short time," he said. "There's no need to explain, I think."

"The den should be Adam's bedroom because Mrs. Frank wants Jane to have her own room," I said. "Now, with even one more person —"

"Yes, yes," Father Matt said. "I hadn't forgotten. Mrs. Frank will understand."

"They never understand anything," I said, sick with misery. "You'd better promise that you'll do it this weekend." The knot in my stomach was growing larger.

"Yes, yes," Father Matt said. Now he was wringing his hands. "You're right. What would I do without my genius Mary Jack?"

He could find out soon enough, I thought, despairing.

Promptly at four, Mrs. Frank rang the doorbell. Adam answered, his hands clean for once. He and Father Matt talked about their plans for the den. I talked about Jane's drawings and how seldom she wet her pants these days. Nobody mentioned Mrs. Bradshaw. Mrs. Frank wrote in her notebook, and left just as Mrs. Percy got home.

They exchanged fake smiles on the porch, reminding me of two people who don't like each other but have to give each other gifts at Christmas anyway.

"I didn't know you were coming," Mrs. Percy said, with a smile spread over her accusation, like jam on cold, dry toast. "I had a faculty meeting."

"Sorry I missed you," Mrs. Frank said, dripping honey, relieved to escape before she had to hear another boring story about how successfully Mrs. Percy helped me with my homework. (I wasn't sure Mrs. Percy even knew what grade I was in.)

We all waved and Mrs. Frank's car pulled away from the curb.

A puddle formed at Jane's feet.

"Oh, great," Adam said bitterly. "I thought we'd get some notice before the flood."

"No," Father Matt said, working hard not to smile, "it's supposed to trickle for a while first."

Both of them laughed, but Mrs. Percy slammed the closet door, then the kitchen door, and finally the door to the cupboard where the glasses were kept. She needed a nerve pill again, I suppose.

We passed one hurdle, but that would be all. Father Matt brought his sister to the house that evening, and ready or not, Adam moved into the den. Then the real troubles began.

Do adults know how their quarrels affect children? I suppose not, or they would keep them a secret. Can't they remember from their own lives how it is to hear people shouting, threatening divorce, issuing orders? Can't they remember the fear that curls children's spines? The lumps in their throats? The little half-moons that fingernails cut into palms? The nights when sleep is impossible because of the angry voices — or the memory of angry voices?

If I ever have children, I won't quarrel where they can hear me. No, not ever.

Father Matt and Mrs. Percy argued more often after Mrs. Bradshaw came. Father Matt, as always, kept his voice so low that I could never be certain of what he said. But Mrs. Percy shouted even louder than before, and I wondered if Mrs. Bradshaw heard — or even if she understood. In some ways, she was like Jane.

Mrs. Bradshaw had three moods, and each of them angered Mrs. Percy. If she was silent — blank as plain paper, really — then Mrs. Percy said she couldn't stand having another person around who didn't talk and couldn't hear. Jane was burden enough.

If Mrs. Bradshaw was cheerful, Mrs. Percy complained about the way she mixed up words, and the way she laughed at things that only children thought were funny — a bird in a tree scolding a cat on the sidewalk, or the way I made a bracelet for Jane from a curl of apple peel.

"We'll call it Jane's *brapplet*," Mrs. Bradshaw said, and I didn't think her brain made a mistake that time.

Sometimes she would talk about her childhood, when she and Father Matt spent their summers at a cabin in the woods and gathered berries (she called them "happies" once, but somehow I knew what she meant). She remembered those times better than anything that had happened the day before. And during those moments, she forgot about the accident.

But on the days she remembered that her husband was dead, and she wasn't able to give piano lessons now because of her concussion, she cried, silently and terribly, for hours at a time. Then Mrs. Percy stayed in her room, with the lights out and a cloth over her forehead. Late at night she would quarrel with Father Matt about *unbearable burdens.*

"I have endless unbearable burdens that are driving me mad," she'd always say. I knew she meant us.

Near the end of May, Mrs. Percy found a solution, and without consulting Mrs. Frank, or even Father Matt, she made arrangements for Mrs. Bradshaw, Adam, Jane, and me to move to the cabin that Father Matt's mother had left Mrs. Bradshaw when she died.

I couldn't help but hear the Percys arguing about it in the dining room, directly below the bedroom Jane and I shared.

"But they can't be there by themselves," Father Matt protested. "Cecile can't take care of the children. She can't even take care of herself. Not yet, anyway."

"I've worked out everything with Gerry," Mrs. Percy said. "She'll stay at the cabin with them for three weeks. We can afford that much. Then we'll think of something else."

"You'll be on your summer break by then," Father Matt said, his voice filled with hope. "You could stay with them. The country air, the clean water. They would do you good."

"No!" Mrs. Percy said. "The children are your problem. Cecile is your sister, not mine. You wanted them. You stay with them."

"But I can't!" said Father Matt. "The cabin is a two-hour drive from the church."

Silence. Somewhere in the neighborhood a dog barked. A car passed the house and turned the corner. I held my breath.

"Jill?" Father Matt said. "You know I can't."

"They go to the cabin for the summer, or I leave this house forever," Mrs. Percy said. "Then you'll lose the children, too."

Jane slipped out of her bed and slid under it. I rolled over in mine and pulled my pillow over my head.

Bad luck made the decision for Father Matt. Gerry's husband ran off, leaving her without enough money to pay her rent, and so when Mrs. Percy extended her offer to include a whole summer at the mountain cabin, all expenses paid and a small salary, too, Gerry didn't have much choice. I guess all those other jobs were filled.

Adam and I were taken out of school two weeks

before summer vacation officially began. Our clothes were packed, along with Jane's and Mrs. Bradshaw's, into Father Matt's old station wagon, and on a sunny Saturday morning, the Percys said goodbye to us.

Mrs. Percy was curt enough. "Try to make yourself useful," she said to me. She said nothing at all to the others.

Father Matt blessed us all, right there on the sidewalk, which was nice, and he gave Gerry an extra thirty dollars in case anybody got hungry during the drive.

Adam crawled into the front of the station wagon next to Gerry. Jane sat in the second seat, between Mrs. Bradshaw and me.

"Where are we going, Matt?" Mrs. Bradshaw asked, her voice filled with sudden alarm.

"To the cabin, Cecile," he said. "Remember? Where we went during the summer when we were children?"

"But aren't you coming, too?" Mrs. Bradshaw asked. Apparently she hadn't remembered anything anyone had told her while we were getting ready to leave.

"I'll come up to see you every Saturday," he said, and he closed the car door next to her. I saw tears glint in his eyes before he turned his head away.

My worries buzzed in my head like insects. This wouldn't work. I'd stayed in a cabin once before, the whole foster family in sleeping bags in one room, with no bathroom and a well for water. That had been only for a week.

A whole summer with Gerry? She was so lazy, so mean. Jane was so delicate. Mrs. Bradshaw was so sick.

And Adam was sure to run away.

Gerry started the car and headed toward the freeway. I clenched my fists and tasted salt water.

Suddenly, Mrs. Bradshaw spoke and made sense. "It's good we don't have anything heavy to carry, except for the groceries," she said. "We'll have to walk about a quarter of a mile."

Gerry's head swiveled on her fat neck. "What do you mean, walk?" she demanded as she slammed on the brakes.

"Why," Mrs. Bradshaw said, smiling, "when the road ends, we take the path on the left and walk to the river. That's where the cabin is."

Adam laughed abruptly and fell silent. The car lurched ahead, and Jane leaned against me, sucking her thumb.

"There's a place to park the car," Mrs. Bradshaw told Gerry. "Right there at the end of the road."

I hugged Jane tightly. A path when the road ends, leading to a cabin on a river. A long summer, when anything might happen.

"There are twelve kinds of berries growing there in the woods," Mrs. Bradshaw said.

Twelve kinds of *happies*? I doubted it.

CHAPTER 3

Mrs. Bradshaw didn't like riding in a car, and traffic on the freeway north of Seattle was bad that bright Saturday morning. It didn't get much better when we turned off on a narrow highway running east through a long, green valley, heading toward the Cascade Mountains. Mrs. Bradshaw never said a word after we left town, but her hands trembled, and she kept her eyes shut.

We'd been on the road for an hour and a half when Jane began squirming.

"Gerry, Jane has to use a bathroom," I said as I leaned forward, close to the driver's seat.

"We can't stop," Gerry snarled.

"Stop the car!" Adam said. "I'm hungry and it's nearly noon. The priest said we could stop to eat."

"We're almost at the cabin," Gerry said.

"Jane has to go to the bathroom now!" I cried. "She'll wet her pants in the car!"

"If she does, she'll get what she deserves," Gerry said.

Why wouldn't she stop? The car seemed to go even faster, hurtling toward the slate blue line of mountains ahead of us.

"Jeez, you really *are* nuts," Adam told Gerry.

"Watch your mouth." Gerry hunched over the wheel.

Mrs. Bradshaw seemed to be dozing, but suddenly her eyes opened and she said, "I insist that you stop this car at the next place where there's likely to be a rest room."

Her voice rang with authority, and no one was more astonished than Gerry, whose head swiveled on her neck again, as if she needed to be certain that the speaker had really been Mrs. Bradshaw.

Gerry couldn't see Mrs. Bradshaw's hands shaking, but I could. Her eyes closed again, and her mouth tightened, as if she was afraid she'd start crying. I was afraid she would, too.

Gerry pulled up at a roadside restaurant, and I hurried Jane inside to the rest room. She wasn't wet, so I hugged and praised her for controlling herself during those bad moments in the car.

When we came out of the rest room, we saw Adam and Mrs. Bradshaw sitting in a booth. Adam was reading the menu to Mrs. Bradshaw, who still couldn't see very well. She didn't seem to be listening.

Gerry sat at the counter, away from the rest of us,

26

as if we might, at any moment, embarrass her. Jane and Mrs. Bradshaw had problems, but they weren't noisy ones that would draw a crowd. I had never liked Gerry, but now I hated her. I'd hoped I could count on her for help, but now I knew that I couldn't.

I slid into the booth next to Mrs. Bradshaw. "Jane's hungry, too, I bet," I said. "What are you going to order?"

Mrs. Bradshaw looked blankly at me, then at Adam. "I'm so sorry," she said quietly, "but I don't think I know where I am."

"Jeez, not again," Adam said. He bent over the menu, ignoring us.

"We're in a restaurant, on our way to the cabin where you spent your summers a long time ago." I spoke softly, hoping that she'd understand me. I'd never felt more alone in my life.

Mrs. Bradshaw nodded and folded her hands in her lap. "I'd like a turkey sandwich and a cup of coffee," she said.

Adam let out the breath he'd been holding. "I'll have a hamburger and a milk shake."

I reached for the menu, and when the waitress came, I ordered turkey sandwiches for Jane and me, too, and milk. I watched the woman's face closely. I was sure she thought we were only another family, on the road for a Saturday outing. Both Jane and Mrs. Bradshaw looked just like regular people.

At the counter, Gerry gobbled her food, not glancing anywhere but at her plate. She had all the money. Would she remember that she was supposed to pay for us? I wasn't certain, so I left the booth and told her that we'd ordered.

She didn't look up.

"You have the money," I said. "You have to pay."

She hesitated a moment too long, just long enough to scare me. Then she nodded. I skipped back to the booth.

"It's okay," I told Adam.

After we'd finished eating and the waitress brought our check, Mrs. Bradshaw automatically opened her purse and pulled out a wallet. She stared at the folded paper money I didn't know she had, and, strangely, her eyes filled with tears.

"Gerry's paying," I said. "You can put your money away."

She didn't seem to hear me. Instead, she studied the money, and then looked helplessly at me. "I'm not sure how . . ."

Adam groaned aloud. "Listen," he said to the waitress, "that fat lady at the counter will pay our check. Give it to her."

"Who says?" the waitress demanded. She was gawking at Mrs. Bradshaw.

"The lady at the counter is paying for all of us," I said quickly, but then, to my horror, I saw Gerry plop down off her stool and waddle toward the door. "Gerry!" I shouted.

Everybody but Gerry stared at me. She charged out the door toward the car, her fat shoulders drawn up around her ears.

"Adam, catch her!" I cried, terrified that Gerry would leave us behind.

Adam sprinted toward the door, and I watched through the window while he caught up with Gerry, grabbing at her arm. They argued for a moment, then Adam snatched the car keys out of her hand and ran back to us.

Breathing hard, he slid back into his seat. "Mrs. Bradshaw, we'll get this straightened out in a minute. But right now I need money to pay the waitress." He picked up the check and read off the total to us.

The waitress couldn't take her gaze off Mrs. Bradshaw, who was weeping silently, her face so white that I was afraid she'd faint.

"I'll help you," I said to her, and I took the wallet from her nerveless fingers. Quickly I counted out enough money to pay the waitress. My thoughts frightened me — Mrs. Bradshaw didn't remember money.

Was this the reason she hadn't been eating when she was living alone in her apartment? She didn't know how to get food? But she was supposed to be recovering! Father Matt had said so.

This was worse than my nightmares. We were supposed to stay at the cabin all summer. But Gerry wouldn't. No matter what she had promised Father

29

Matt, I knew she wouldn't stay. And then what would happen? We couldn't live at the cabin with only Mrs. Bradshaw watching over us — she needed more care than Jane!

We'd be taken back to Seattle, separated, and sent off to new foster homes. Poor Jane, starting all over again, maybe with no one like me to help. And another foster father might not be as tolerant of Adam as Father Matt.

I was tired of lying to myself, telling myself again and again that this time I had a real home, a real family, a place where I could stay forever, maybe even until I was grown up myself.

Perhaps there was some way I could make friends with Gerry, persuade her to stay with us. In the fall, when the time came for school to start, Mrs. Percy might not be so nervous. She'd have had the whole summer to herself. Things might still work out. After all, Father Matt had said that Mrs. Bradshaw's concussion would heal, and she could live alone again. By the end of summer, Jane might be talking. And Adam — well, he could leave or stay.

I grabbed Jane's hand and said, "Come on, everybody, let's get started."

Mrs. Bradshaw followed us, obedient as a dog. Adam trotted ahead, jittery with nervous energy.

Gerry stood beside the station wagon, glowering. When Adam handed her the keys, she unlocked her own door and then, begrudgingly, let the rest of us in through the other doors.

"You take the keys again and you'll be sorry," she said to Adam.

Adam didn't respond, but I knew from his expression that her threats meant nothing to him.

The sun was hot for May. The higher we climbed into the mountains, the warmer we got. Finally, when we saw a sign that pointed to Monarch River, we left the highway for a winding road that cut through a cool forest. I smelled cedar trees.

"Are we getting close?" I asked Mrs. Bradshaw.

"Yes," she said. "We'll stop at the store in Monarch River for milk. And fresh vegetables and fruit."

A knot inside me untied gently and I relaxed against the seat. She sounded as if she was remembering things better now.

But a mile farther along, when we saw the village ahead, I knew that Mrs. Bradshaw was remembering only the past.

"Where's the store?" she cried as we passed a vacant lot next to a gas station.

"Down the street," Adam said, pointing ahead to a small, modern grocery store.

But Mrs. Bradshaw was looking behind us at the vacant lot. "Where's the store?" she repeated.

"Stop!" Adam shouted at Gerry, because she was driving past the new store.

She stopped, but she was angry. "Father Matt put a box full of stuff in the back," she said. "I'd like to know who's going to carry more groceries to this cabin if the road stops before we get there."

"We only have enough food to last a couple of days," I said. "I heard Father Matt say that we'd have to stop for more."

"Then you'll carry it," Gerry said.

"Get out of the car with us," Adam said to her. "You should have paid for lunch. Now you'd better pay for the food or I'll phone the priest."

Gerry shot him a poisonous look, but she got out and followed us to the store.

Inside, Mrs. Bradshaw looked around with such bewilderment that I felt sorry for her.

"It's okay," I whispered. "It's just a new store. Don't worry about it."

She didn't seem to recognize the man behind the counter, so maybe, I thought, he hadn't been the owner of the old store. Even better, the man didn't recognize her. If he'd known her, and she hadn't remembered him, we'd be faced with another awful moment.

Gerry took milk out of the refrigerator, bread from a shelf, and would have stopped there if I hadn't reminded her that we needed a salad for dinner, and butter. The cabin had a refrigerator, Father Matt had said.

"Let's get orange juice, too," I told Gerry.

She glared at me. The man behind the counter tried to strike up a conversation with Mrs. Bradshaw, but she didn't answer his pleasantries, and only stared out his window at the street.

Adam responded instead, and I could tell that he was afraid we'd attract the wrong kind of attention.

"Yes, we're from Seattle," he said, answering a question.

"You out of school already?" the man asked.

"Sure," Adam said. "So we're spending a few days at our cabin."

"That so?" the man asked. He rang up our groceries on his cash register. "At the river or farther down the valley?"

Adam looked helplessly at Mrs. Bradshaw, but she was unaware. Gerry answered instead. "The cabin's on the river," she said, and she thrust money at him.

The man looked curiously at Mrs. Bradshaw, shrugged a little, and said, "Well, you'll have it to yourself for a while. The summer people don't come until June."

"We're used to it," Adam lied. He grabbed the grocery sacks and hurried toward the door.

Gerry followed, leaving me to deal with Jane and Mrs. Bradshaw. I took Jane's hand and touched Mrs. Bradshaw's shoulder.

"But I don't understand where the —" she began.

"Let's hurry," I said. "Jane's ready for a nap."

I glanced back once, and saw with relief that the

man wasn't watching us leave. Perhaps he hadn't thought that anything about us was strange. Maybe I worried too much.

Gerry consulted Father Matt's written instructions before she started the car. "A half mile down River Road," she said aloud.

"When the road ends, we park the car —" Mrs. Bradshaw began.

"Father Matt didn't write that," Gerry said, scowling at Mrs. Bradshaw.

"What did he write?" Adam asked.

Gerry studied the paper, still scowling. "We're to go a half mile down River Road. I thought the cabin was on River Road."

"No, that's when —" Mrs. Bradshaw began again.

"I heard you!" Gerry cried, shrill and red-faced. She started the car and we drove slowly down the street, past a library, a post office, a feed store, and two small restaurants. In the next block, we passed a school, then the volunteer fire department. Ours was the only car moving.

"With all this heavy traffic, they ought to put up some signal lights," Adam said, snickering.

Now we passed houses, old and neat behind low fences and blooming roses.

"Are you watching the mileage?" Adam demanded.

"We're not even on River Road!" Gerry exclaimed. "Can't you read the signs?"

We found River Road, leading off to the left. Gerry turned the car, muttering, "At last."

"Now watch your mileage," Adam said.

"You don't need to watch," Mrs. Bradshaw said, her voice so calm that once again I wondered about the strangeness of her head injury. One moment she sounded as if she remembered everything and the next she couldn't even recall how to use money. "The road simply ends after half a mile."

She was right. We stopped in a wide turnaround. Two paths led off from it, one to the right and the other to the left. Each followed a line of poles carrying wires.

The cabin I had stayed in before had electricity — one naked bulb that lit up the single room. I tried to imagine living with four people in one room for a whole summer. I would manage because I had to manage.

We climbed out of the car and looked at each other.

"Listen," Mrs. Bradshaw said.

We listened. From the distance, I heard a muffled roar.

"The river?" I asked, thrilled at the sound.

She nodded, her face lighted with a smile. "Let's hurry," she said. "Get our things out of the car and hurry."

She carried her own suitcase in her good, right hand and strode off ahead of us. Gerry followed, holding her suitcase in one hand and her purse in the other, leaving Adam, Jane, and me to manage the rest.

"I'll come back for my clothes," Adam said as he lifted the grocery sacks. "I'll bring yours, too, if you take the rest of the food now."

His cooperation astonished me. "Are you sure?" I asked.

His scowl served as an answer to my silly question, but he added, "Our clothes won't spoil in the heat, but the food might."

I didn't have a free hand, so as we walked along the soft path, Jane hung onto the hem of my shirt.

"Isn't this a pretty place?" I asked her, as we followed the electric line through the woods, past blooming dogwood and wild flowers, under drooping branches where birds watched us. Moss silenced our footsteps. We passed a pond, as dark and still as a mirror beneath the trees.

Ahead of us, I saw the cabin. Only it was more than a cabin. It was a beautiful, low house made of logs, with a thick, mossy roof and many windows.

Adam looked back over his shoulder at us. He was grinning.

I grinned, too. "Hey, Jane," I said. "We're home."

Overhead, high in the flat blue sky, an eagle cried out once, twice, as it circled over the river that rushed between great boulders on the other side of the cabin.

Jane looked up at the eagle, then at me. She didn't smile, but her black eyes danced.

Gerry had unlocked the door, and Mrs. Bradshaw was already inside. I could see her through the many-paned windows.

"I'll bet it doesn't even have a TV," Gerry said.

Above us, the eagle cried again, and drifted lazily on air. Who cares about TV? I thought. We have our own eagle.

Mrs. Bradshaw appeared at the door. "Come inside, children," she said. "My mother isn't here right now, but she'll be so glad to see you."

"Jeez," Adam moaned, giving me a significant glance, and he walked in the front door.

Jane looked up at me, anxious, her lower lip trembling.

"It's all right," I said. "Don't worry."

But suddenly I was more scared than I had ever been.

◄ CHAPTER 4 ►

No one had used the cabin for a long time. The furniture in the main room was covered with grimy sheets, and our shoes left clean prints on the dusty floors. In the kitchen, the counters were hidden beneath old sheets of newspaper.

"This place even smells deserted," Adam muttered as he shoved open a window to let in fresh air.

"Come and see your bedrooms," Mrs. Bradshaw called out from the far side of the main room. She sounded happy. Amazing.

I took Jane by the hand, and Adam followed. We found two musty bedrooms, each with two sets of bunks. All eight beds were covered with sheets, dust, and cobwebs.

Between those rooms, a large, cold bathroom opened into the hall. Everything smelled of mice and mildew. But everywhere there were windows that looked into the deep spring woods or over the wild river.

"I'm not cleaning this mess up," Gerry announced.

"You won't have to," I babbled. She couldn't leave! "Adam and I can do it. Jane will help."

I ignored Adam's astonished stare and started pulling sheets off the two sofas in the long main room.

"Wait!" Mrs. Bradshaw cried. "Not like that. Mama wants us to roll them up carefully so the dust doesn't spill. Then we'll carry them outside and shake them."

She was lost in time again. I watched while she, using only her good arm, rolled up the sheets that covered the sofas. Her *mama* said? Didn't she remember that she was grown-up now? That her mother had died and left her this place?

"Come on, Gerry, Mary Jack," she said. "Help with the sheets on the chairs."

I was so grateful that she remembered my name that I nearly forgot that Gerry had to be coaxed into staying, no matter what the cost. "Gerry, sit down and rest for a while," I said. "You must be tired from all that driving."

Gerry sat, without speaking, and watched Mrs. Bradshaw and me uncover the furniture, her mean little eyes unblinking. Jane followed me, close as my shadow. Adam folded the newspapers in the kitchen and came in holding them.

"What do I do with these?" he asked.

Mrs. Bradshaw said, "We'll burn a few at a time in the fireplace, in the evenings when we need a fire."

"I'm not cooking over a fireplace," Gerry said, sullen and purposely disagreeable.

Mrs. Bradshaw straightened up to regard her with a cold, level stare. "Of course not. We have a perfectly good electric range."

Adam reached for a wall switch and clicked it. The ceiling lights came on. I sighed with relief, and I could see that Adam was grateful, too.

"But there's no telephone, no television set," Gerry whined.

"We've never had a phone," Mrs. Bradshaw said. "And we always bring a TV from the city, but I guess we forgot this time. Maybe Matt will bring one when he comes to visit Saturday."

Now she sounded as if she was completely well, and for an hour or so, I was filled with hope. But then later, after the quarrel over the beds, she slipped into blankness again.

It began like this. Adam got the car keys from Gerry and walked to the road to get our clothes. When he returned, he put our bags down and said, "Since there are four beds in each bedroom, which room do you females want?"

I looked at Mrs. Bradshaw for a decision, but Gerry snapped, "Father Matt promised me a room to myself."

Adam flipped his hair away from his face. "You mean I sleep on a sofa?"

"Suit yourself," Gerry said. "Sleep outside, for all I care."

"That's ridiculous," Mrs. Bradshaw told her. "You sleep in the front bedroom with the girls and me."

"No," Gerry said. "Father Matt promised —"

"You'll do as I say," Mrs. Bradshaw said, her voice sharp as a slap on the face. "That child can't sleep on the sofa."

"Father Matt —" Gerry began stubbornly.

Mrs. Bradshaw turned on her. "Listen to me! Adam sleeps in the back bedroom and that's final. Don't say another word, because I won't put up with your attitude, you rotten *idiot*."

Only she didn't say idiot. She said the bad *F* word instead.

Gerry was stunned into silence, and Jane cringed behind me. But Adam burst out laughing. From that moment on he changed how he behaved toward Mrs. Bradshaw. Maybe it took her swearing for him to see that she had something in common with him — nobody wanted her, either, and that can make a person very angry.

Gerry shut up then, but her face turned so dark a purple that for a while I thought she'd be sick. After a few minutes, she told Adam to give her back the car keys, and she dropped them in her purse, then lumbered into the front bedroom and slammed the door.

I hoped that she'd make the beds with the sheets

and blankets we'd found in the closet, but I knew better than to count on it.

Mrs. Bradshaw, still a little shaky from her argument with Gerry, helped Jane and me put groceries away in the kitchen. She even remembered how to turn on the refrigerator and hot water heater. But then, gradually, she became confused again, until finally she stood in the middle of the kitchen, holding an empty sack, and didn't know what to do next. I took her arm and walked into the main room with her.

"What's wrong?" Adam asked quickly. He'd been sweeping the dust from the floor the way she'd taught him, with a damp broom.

"She's just tired," I said, hoping I was right.

Gerry had waddled back out to sit on a sofa and watch Adam work. "She's flipped out again," she said. She heaved herself to her feet. "Now I suppose *I* have to fix dinner."

"It's what you were hired to do!" Adam shouted.

I shot him a panicky look, but he didn't read it right. His scowl grew only more fierce, and he jammed his hands in his pockets. "She's supposed to do the cooking," he said to me.

"But she's tired," I said. "Gerry, I'll help. I can make the salad and set the table."

But Gerry stomped into the kitchen without looking at me.

I followed her, but Jane lingered behind, watching Mrs. Bradshaw. A few minutes later, when I looked in on them, I saw that Jane had taken her tablet and crayons from her bag and was sitting on the floor at Mrs. Bradshaw's feet, drawing.

Mrs. Bradshaw's eyes were shut and her cheeks wet with tears. I didn't know if she was crying from frustration or despair.

Ordinarily Adam would have been rolling his eyes and sighing, but this time I saw him standing in the open doorway, looking out into the woods, calmly pretending that everything was all right, that he wasn't in the same room with a weeping woman and a child who couldn't — or wouldn't — speak.

When dinner was on the table, Mrs. Bradshaw didn't come to the kitchen. I don't know if she even heard me when I told her it was ready. On her lap lay the drawing Jane had made.

Curious, I picked it up. There were four figures in front of a long, brown house. One figure, a boy, had straight blond hair. One had long brown hair, and I knew that was Mrs. Bradshaw. There was the usual figure representing me. And a funny, short one with a fat face and turned-down mouth. Gerry. I bit my lip to keep from laughing and put the drawing back on Mrs. Bradshaw's lap.

"It's a funny picture," I whispered to her. "I know you'd feel better if you looked at it."

She heard me. I knew because she shook her head a little.

"Try," I whispered. "It would make Jane so happy."

Mrs. Bradshaw opened her eyes and looked down at the drawing. Then she raised her hand and covered one eye — I'd seen her do that at Father Matt's house when she needed to see something clearly. He said it was because she still had double vision. Suddenly she smiled and looked up at me, then pointed at the fat-faced figure.

"She's such a —" she said.

"I know," I whispered quickly before she used the *F* word again. "Don't you want to eat with us?"

She shook her head and closed her eyes. But her good hand was holding the drawing and she was still smiling.

Jane and Adam had been watching from the kitchen door. Adam grinned, and I thought that perhaps Jane was standing a little closer to him than she had ever dared before. But I couldn't be certain. Men and boys bothered Jane more than women and girls did.

Gerry had fixed macaroni and cheese from a box, and it actually was good. We had salami and bread, and my salad, of course. All of us were hungry — because of the country air, Adam said.

Gerry said nothing at all, and when she was done eating, she got up from the table and left the room.

"Don't say anything about the dishes," I told Adam. "I'll do them. We don't want to make her so mad that she'll leave us here."

"Who cares?" Adam asked.

"You'll care as much as I do, if we have to go back to the city and Mrs. Percy won't let us live in the house again," I said. "It's not a bad foster home. Things could be worse. And this cabin is nicer than I thought it would be. We can spend the summer here just fine, if Gerry doesn't leave. But we can't stay here with only Mrs. Bradshaw. You know that."

"Maybe she'll get better."

"Maybe not," I said. "I don't think Father Matt would have sent Gerry along if there was a real chance that Mrs. Bradshaw could manage everything."

Adam pushed his plate away. "Yeah."

He didn't help me with the dishes, but he did ask Mrs. Bradshaw if she felt well enough to walk down to the river with him. I told Jane to go, too, but she walked only as far as the porch, where she sat down on a step and hugged her tablet to her chest.

Gerry had found an old radio in a cupboard, and she plugged it in and turned it to a loud station.

After I put the last dish away, I walked down to the river, too, bringing Jane along. Adam and Mrs. Bradshaw were sitting on a slab of rock under a tree, both of them watching the sky. The eagle was back, drifting in lazy circles.

"Don't get too close to the river," I told Jane, even

though she didn't seem anxious to let go of my hand.

"It's shallow," Adam said. He held up his bare feet for me to see. "I waded across to the other side. It's rocky, but it's not deep enough to drown her."

"In the winter," Mrs. Bradshaw began, and she shook her head warningly. "In the winter . . ." But she forgot what she was going to say, and looked up at the eagle again, squinting against the late afternoon sun.

"In the winter, the river would be high and maybe dangerous," Adam said. "But we won't be here then."

Jane pretended that she didn't hear him, but she let go of my hand and sat cautiously on the rock next to Mrs. Bradshaw, leaning against her a little.

Adam pulled on his socks and shoes. "What's Gerry doing?"

"Listening to the radio she found," I said.

"In the bedroom?"

"No, in the main room," I said. "Why?"

"Be back in a while," he said, and he sprinted around toward the back of the cabin, where the bedroom windows were open wide so that the rooms could air out.

I supposed that he wanted something from his room and didn't want to pass Gerry for fear she'd start an argument. I saw him climb in his window, and then I turned back to Mrs. Bradshaw.

46

"Are there fish in the river?" I asked.

"Yes," she said. "And in the pond. There are ducks in the pond, too. And the moonstones come there."

"What?" I asked, and then could have bitten my tongue, because when I looked at her, I saw that she'd said a wrong word again, and her face was twisted with embarrassment.

"Moonstones," she repeated, then shook her head, angry with herself. "No."

Jane looked up at her, curious.

Mrs. Bradshaw's eyes glinted. "Moon . . ."

"Moonlight?" I asked.

"No, moonracks," she said. "No!"

"Raccoons," I cried, inspired finally by her efforts.

She burst out laughing. "Yes. Stupid me. Sometimes I know the right word here," and she touched her head, "but the wrong word comes out here." She touched her mouth.

"Aphasia," I said. "I had a foster father once who had that, after he had a stroke. But you didn't have a stroke."

"No," she said. "A concussion. I'll get well. But maybe never. A long never." And her eyes glinted again.

I bent my head and rested it on my knees so that she couldn't see my face. This was terrible. How could I bear it? A whole summer of her craziness, and Gerry's meanness, and Jane's silence, and Adam's sarcasm. Sometimes I was scared of being so scared.

Adam was back, whistling under his breath. He sat down on another rock and looked up at the sky, empty now. The eagle had disappeared.

"What did you get from your room?" I asked.

"Nothing," he said.

"Then why did you climb in the window?"

He pulled the car keys out of his pocket. "This is easier than locking her in her bedroom tonight," he said.

"You think she'll run off?" I asked, panicked.

"I know she will," he said. "She's waiting until dark. Then she thinks she'll get in the car and take off." He laughed, and stuck the keys back in his pocket.

"She'll be mad," I predicted.

"Who cares? What's she going to do, phone the priest from Monarch River and tell him I took the keys so she can't run away and leave us here? Remember, she's got a lot of cash — I saw the priest give it to her. With that and a car, she could have gone a long way."

"She wouldn't have dared," I said. "Father Matt would have sent the police after her."

Adam turned to look at me. "Are you kidding? He'd pray about it, that's all."

He was right. I clenched my fists so hard that my nails dug in my palms. Sooner or later Gerry would miss her keys, even if she hadn't planned to abandon us. Then what?

We stayed outside until the mosquitoes bothered us too much, and Jane was half asleep. When we went indoors, Gerry was fixing herself a sandwich in the kitchen. She had the radio with her. She didn't say anything to us and we didn't talk to her.

I gave Jane a quick bath and tucked her into a top bunk because I remembered how much I liked sleeping in one when I was her age. Then, reluctantly, I went out into the main room.

Adam had built a small fire. Gerry was eating cookies from a sack. The door was closed, and the dark woods pressed against the house. After a while, Mrs. Bradshaw went to bed, but first she warned Adam to make sure the fire was out before he left the room.

Gerry turned the radio from station to station, never listening to anything for very long. She seemed nervous, and that made me nervous. At last the fire went out and Adam went to his room.

"I guess I'll go to bed now, too," I said to Gerry. "It must be pretty late. How about you?"

"I'm not tired," she said.

She's going to try running away, I thought. What will she do when she learns that the keys are gone from her purse? She'll be furious.

But what can she actually do?

I went to bed and lay awake in the other top bunk for a long time, listening to the radio in the main room. Jane slept in spite of the music — I could hear her soft, even breathing. Even Mrs. Bradshaw slept, although once or twice she whimpered in dreams, but I didn't think that she woke herself.

Then I heard a soft scraping on the floor. I turned my head so that I could see the door. Gerry stood there, very still, looking from one bunk to the other to see if anyone was awake. I hardly dared breathe.

She moved another two steps into the room and lifted her purse from the dresser. And then, slowly, she bent to pick up the suitcase that she had never unpacked.

Adam was right. But what would she do when she found out that she didn't have the car keys?

I listened while she left the house, not even closing the front door behind her. After a long time, I got up and went to the room next to ours.

"Adam, are you awake?" I whispered.

"I heard her go," he said in a normal voice. And then he laughed.

"Shouldn't she be back by now? I mean, she must know that she doesn't have the keys."

"She's probably standing out there in the woods, trying to figure out what to do," he said.

"But what if she doesn't come back?" I asked. "What if she walks somewhere and hitches a ride or catches a bus?"

"She's too fat to walk far," Adam said. "But who cares? Let me get some sleep."

I lay awake all night long, and Gerry didn't return.

In the morning, when the first pale light filled our windows, I knew that I wouldn't have the Percys for a real family, either.

"She didn't come back, did she?" Mrs. Bradshaw said from the bunk under mine.

I jerked upright. "What?" I said. "You knew?"

"Oh, yes," Mrs. Bradshaw said. "Good riddance."

Adam stuck his head in our room. "Is it too early for breakfast?" he asked.

And so began our adventure.

❧ CHAPTER 5 ❧

The four of us gathered in the kitchen that Sunday morning as soon as we had dressed.

"Let's have pancakes," Adam said, and he sounded excited in a strange, nervous way.

"I know how to make them," I said, doing my best to seem confident instead of scared.

"Jane and I will set the table," Mrs. Bradshaw said.

Then we looked at each other, and the three of us began laughing. It didn't make much sense, and I couldn't believe we were doing it.

"We're in awful trouble," I said finally. "Gerry will tell Father Matt and Mrs. Percy."

"No way." Adam shook his head. "Then the priest would know that she abandoned us."

"She'll think up an excuse," I said. "He'll come here in the other car and get us, as soon as church services are over."

Mrs. Bradshaw reached out her good hand and

placed it on Jane's thin shoulder. "We'll *card* with it . . ." she began. Then she frowned, said, "No!" and began again. "We'll . . ."

"Deal with it," Adam supplied, with patience he didn't usually show her.

She nodded. "Don't worry."

But I was heavy with dread, and I moved so slowly mixing the pancake batter that I thought I'd be in the kitchen until noon. I spilled things, dropped a measuring cup, and finally turned to Adam, who was filling glasses with the last of our milk.

I said, "If Gerry tells Father Matt that we were too awful to stay with, and Mrs. Percy won't let us go back, then we'll be split up and sent to other foster homes this week."

Adam shrugged. "I'll survive."

"But Jane will be scared." From where I stood, I could see Mrs. Bradshaw giving Jane a lesson in setting a table. "She hid under her bed all day when she first came to the Percys' house," I said.

"Everybody survives," Adam said, his voice gruff. "Everybody." He wouldn't look at me.

I poured batter into the frying pan, making a pancake shaped like a teddy bear for Jane. Adam was right. But that didn't mean the survivors were happy. I had a hunch that he knew a lot about just barely hanging on. But he was mean enough not to care if Jane had to hang on forever. I didn't talk again until I brought the pancakes to the table.

"Breakfast," I said.

Mrs. Bradshaw, who'd been watching the river out the window, turned and stared. "Ah, Mary Jack," she said, as if she'd forgotten I was there. Her bad hand, the one that didn't work right, was trembling, and I was sure that she wasn't aware of it.

Oh, this was all hopeless!

I spread jam on Jane's pancake and cut it up for her. Mrs. Bradshaw managed with one hand to pour syrup on her pancakes and cut them with a fork. Adam gobbled a stack silently, washing it down with orange juice. No one spoke until we were through eating.

Then Mrs. Bradshaw said, "I have a plan."

I was astonished. Sometimes, when Mrs. Bradshaw was silent for a long time, I suspected that nothing at all was going on in her brain, that her mind was like a blank page in Jane's tablet. "What plan?" I asked.

"If Gerry goes to my brother, we'll ask to stay here by ourselves on a trial basis," she said. "We'll invite Matt back to check on us next Saturday and see how we're doing. How does that sound?"

"Sounds good to me," Adam said, leaning forward and resting on his elbows.

"Sure," I said, smiling as if I believed it was possible. I was trying hard not to watch Mrs. Bradshaw's hand tremble.

"I can't drive yet," she said, "but we don't need

Gerry for that. We can walk to town when we need things."

I remembered when she looked in her wallet and didn't know what money was. And I remembered that she didn't have much of it, either. "Did Gerry take the money Father Matt gave her?" I asked.

"Probably," Adam said. "But I'll look around the house for it anyway." He bolted off to the bedrooms.

I glanced at Mrs. Bradshaw. "We'll need money for food. If Father Matt comes, you'll have to ask him for more," I said.

"I've got my checkbook," she told me. "Even if he doesn't come, we'll get along fine." But she wasn't smiling any longer. The scar on her forehead burned scarlet. Suddenly she bent her head and tears gushed down her face.

Oh, no! I never knew what to do when she wept.

Jane sat like a stone, her eyes fixed on her plate. I jumped up and led her away from the table. "Let's wash your sticky face and hands," I said.

Jane came willingly enough, and when I'd cleaned her up, she went to our bedroom, passing Adam on the way, and gathered up her tablet and crayons. Then, without looking at any of us, she marched to the main room, sat on the floor, and began drawing.

"Did you find the money?" I asked Adam.

He shook his head. He was prowling in the main room, restless and scowling, opening drawers and feeling along shelves that were over his head, discovering nothing but dust and odd scraps of paper. "Gerry took it. I knew she would."

"Mrs. Bradshaw says she has a checkbook," I told him.

His eyes lighted briefly, but then he shook his head, hard. "Didn't you know she can't write? That's the real reason her landlady called the priest. She couldn't write a check for her rent when the landlady asked for it. The priest had to make it out for her and help her sign her name on the line."

"Then she is mentally retarded."

Adam hunched his shoulders. "The priest said she isn't, that she'll be all right in time. But I never heard of anybody like her turning completely normal."

"Maybe it's different if you were normal to begin with," I said. But I remembered Ben Nickerson, who'd had a stroke. He didn't get better. Not much, anyway.

Adam glanced out the nearest window. "I'm going out for a while," he said.

"Why?" I blurted. Adam might run away, too. I'd always suspected it.

"We need wood," he said. "There's no heat here except for the fireplace, and we burned all the wood in the box last night."

"Promise me that you won't run away, too!"

"Would you believe me?" he asked. "You're crazy

if you believe anybody." And with that, he left the house.

Mrs. Bradshaw still wept, silently, and she didn't seem to be aware of Jane and me. Jane appeared beside me and held up a drawing.

I studied it seriously, the way I always did. Sometimes I could figure out how Jane felt by her pictures.

She'd drawn me, Adam, and Mrs. Bradshaw standing in a room with many windows. Our mouths turned up in smiles. In the doorway of the room, she'd drawn the back of another figure, a fat one. As usual, she didn't appear in her own drawing.

"You're glad Gerry left?" I asked.

Jane only looked at me, but her eyes shone.

"It might not be such a good thing," I said, needing to prepare her so that if we had to go back, she wouldn't be too disappointed. "Father Matt might not like us being here alone."

Her eyes went blank again. She sat in a chair near a window and looked out, ignoring me.

Mrs. Bradshaw's weeping presence disturbed me even more now. I went to her and touched her shoulder. "Don't feel bad," I said. "We'll work everything out. I'm sure of it."

"I'm sorry," she wept. "So very sorry. I'm truly sorry."

She did that sometimes. She apologized over and

over to anybody who was standing around. That was worse than her tears.

"Maybe you should lie down," I suggested. "You could lie here on the sofa and look out the windows. Adam's hunting for firewood. When he gets back, he can make us a fire."

Mrs. Bradshaw wiped her face with the backs of her hands. "Firewood is stored in the shed," she said, her voice breaking. "The door is . . ." She lost track of her words again.

"It's locked?" I asked.

She nodded and pointed toward the mantel. "The locker . . . the locker . . ."

"The key's on the mantel," I said, running across the room and searching among the dusty framed photographs. "Here it is!" I held it up for her to see.

"The key," she said, and she laughed. "I knew that word. Come along and I'll show you the shed."

I followed her outside and blinked in the brilliant sun. There came Adam, staggering under a giant armload of sticks that he'd gathered in the woods.

I wanted to leap around and shout. Adam hadn't run off! But instead, I said, "That's a lot of good kindling. Mrs. Bradshaw says there's more wood in a locked shed in back."

"I thought it was a tool shed," Adam said. He dropped his load of sticks on the porch and followed us.

The padlock on the old door was too stiff for Mrs.

Bradshaw to work, so Adam opened it. Inside the shed, logs cut to the right size were stacked to the roof. A canvas carrier hung from a hook.

"I'm glad I gathered sticks," Adam said. "There's no kindling here."

Mrs. Bradshaw stooped and picked up something wrapped in canvas. She handed it to Adam and said, "For kindling."

Adam unwrapped an axe and shrugged a little. "I'll try it."

"I know how to use it," Mrs. Bradshaw said, "but my arm . . ." She raised her bad arm as far as she could and let it fall back.

"I can chop kindling," Adam said, gruff and scowling.

Mrs. Bradshaw smiled crookedly. "I knew you could," she said.

Adam filled the log carrier and took it into the house. But the morning was growing warmer, and we wouldn't need a fire until much later in the day. And maybe, by evening, we'd be back in Seattle, waiting for someone to take us away from the Percys'.

Until lunch time, we walked on the riverbank, then on a narrow path through the woods to the pond, where wildflowers grew.

"This is called bleeding-heart," Mrs. Bradshaw said, touching a delicate, lavender flower that hung from a slender stalk. "And the small yellow flowers, here under the ferns, are violets."

Jane knelt to look closely at them. When she reached to take one, Mrs. Bradshaw stopped her gently. "It's best not to pick them," she said, sounding like a perfectly normal mother. "We can always come out here to see them."

She showed us trilliums, brilliant white in shaded places, and tiny star flowers nodding on stems as fine as hair. There was Solomon's seal, with its pale green bells, blooming beside the path. And mayflowers, looking like the dogwood blossoms that starred the woods.

She pointed out strawberry and blackcap blossoms, blackberry and wild raspberry, huckleberry, Oregon grape, and more. "The berries will ripen all summer long," she said. "My mother made jams and jellies from them."

Once I saw Adam smile behind her back, a contented smile, the sort I had never seen on his face before.

Jane was growing more confident of Mrs. Bradshaw, walking closer to her, and sometimes not darting away when Mrs. Bradshaw stopped to point out another wonder.

When we reached the pond, a pair of ducks flew off, squawking an alarm. "Poor things," Mrs. Bradshaw said. "They must have a basket here."

Adam burst out laughing. "You mean nest."

"Yes," Mrs. Bradshaw said, and she laughed, too. "For a while I thought I was myself again." She brushed a long strand of hair away from her forehead. "Sometimes I am, almost, but then . . ."

I could see that Adam was uncomfortable with this talk, and so was I. "Maybe we should go back for lunch," I said. "I don't know what time it is, but Jane might be pretty tired."

Adam, the only one of us who had a watch, consulted it and said, "It's twelve-fifteen."

Mrs. Bradshaw started, as if she'd heard a loud noise. "Matt might have come. He might be looking for us."

"Church services were over at twelve," I said. "He'll still be talking to people in the coffee lounge."

"Oh, yes," Mrs. Bradshaw said. "Yes."

"Mrs. Bradshaw," I began, but she didn't let me finish.

"Please don't call me that anymore," she said. "Call me Aunt Cecile. I always wanted nieces and nephews."

"Aunt Cecile," I began again, uncomfortably. "Jane ought to have milk for lunch, but we've used it all. Can you let us have money to buy some in town?" I dreaded asking this, for I was haunted by the problem of money and whether or not she would remember it.

"Of course you may have money," she said. She strode down the path ahead of us, and no one seeing us coming along that path would have thought that there was anything wrong with her.

But when we reached the cabin, she'd forgotten all about money, and I had to ask her again. "If you don't mind," I added. "I can run into town and be back very soon."

She stared blankly at me.

"Money, Aunt Cecile," Adam said. "From your wallet."

"Yes," she said, and she went to her purse, took out the wallet, and handed it to Adam. "You do it."

At least she knew that money was kept in wallets. I wished, desperately, that there was some way to predict what she'd remember and what she wouldn't. And when.

Adam said he'd go to the store with me, because he wanted to check on the car. "And Gerry might be hanging around someplace," he murmured to me on our way out the door.

I'd almost forgotten her. And I didn't have time to worry about her now. "One of us should stay here," I said. "What about Jane? We can't leave her here alone with Aunt Cecile."

"We won't be gone long," Adam protested.

But I went back inside, took Jane to the bathroom, and explained to Aunt Cecile that we were bringing Jane with us so she could get acquainted with the town.

Aunt Cecile's face told me that she knew why we wouldn't leave Jane with her. She nodded, smiling in her lopsided way. "Good," she said. But when she turned away, her whole body sagged. I knew she was ashamed.

I ran with Jane to catch up with Adam, who'd refused to wait. We passed the pond, just in time to frighten off the ducks again, and Adam said "Hey" so disgustedly that I laughed.

"They'll get used to us," I said. Then I remembered that we wouldn't be around long enough to be a problem for the ducks.

When we reached the car, Adam examined it carefully, as if he had expected something to be wrong with it.

"At least she didn't trash it," he said finally. He unlocked the driver's door and sat inside.

"What are you doing?" I asked. "We've got to hurry."

"I could drive us to town," he said.

"You could not," I said. "You're not old enough to drive."

"That doesn't mean I don't know how," he said, turning the steering wheel back and forth. "I drove my mom's car."

"She let you?" I asked, not really believing him.

He stopped turning the wheel, but he didn't answer.

"She didn't know you drove it, did she?" I accused.

He glared at me. "So what?"

"You sneaked out at night and drove it?"

He hesitated a moment too long. "Yeah," he said, bitter and angry again. "While she slept."

I suspected then that his mother was a drunk. I'd known a boy the summer before who took his father's car sometimes, when his father drank so much that he passed out. That boy had been fifteen, a year older than Adam.

"Come on, Adam," I said. "Lock the car and let's go."

He did as I said, which surprised me. It had crossed my mind that Adam could easily get away from us right now, since he knew how to drive. But I hadn't counted on him for anything anyway.

In town, we bought a gallon of milk at the store.

"How's your mother getting along?" the man behind the counter asked. "Is she enjoying herself?"

"She loves it here," I said, ducking my head in case he was good at reading expressions. I'd never been a successful liar.

"You kids behave now," he told us as we left the store.

I looked back, startled, but then I saw that it was just his way of saying goodbye. He wasn't accusing us of anything.

Jane's footsteps dragged on the way home, so I persuaded Adam to carry the milk while I carried Jane. She was too heavy for me, but she wouldn't let Adam touch her. That time when we passed the pond, the ducks quacked, but they didn't fly off.

"Friends at last," Adam said in his sarcastic voice.

I didn't answer. I was too out of breath.

At the cabin, we found Aunt Cecile making sandwiches. "Here you are," she said. "Did everything go all right?"

"Fine," Adam said.

She took the milk from him, and then said, "Adam, I found my father's old clock. See? Would you wind it and set the time? I like to hear a clock ticking. It makes me feel at home."

Adam picked up an old, wood-covered clock from the counter and wound the key in the back, set it, and put it down. Jane stared at it, fascinated.

"Let's put it on the mantel," Aunt Cecile said.

We all watched Adam set it in its proper place. Aunt Cecile was right. A ticking clock did sound good.

I glanced down at Jane and caught her looking up at me. Her eyes sparkled — and she clicked her tongue.

"Hey," I said. "She made a sound like a clock!"

Aunt Cecile laughed and hugged Jane. But Adam, who was determined to be unpleasant, said, "Big deal. Maybe she'll learn to snore next and we can send her to college."

I laughed in spite of myself. "It's a start," I said.

The small clock on the mantel surprised me then with a sound, a little ding.

"It's one-thirty," Aunt Cecile said. "Let's eat."

One-thirty. If Father Matt knew that we'd been deserted, he'd be on his way by now. He might even be halfway to the cabin.

Even though I was hungry, I had a hard time swallowing. Poor Aunt Cecile. She felt at home because of a ticking clock. But the clock was only marking how much time we had left.

CHAPTER 6

We waited all day for Father Matt. When dark fell and it was obvious that he wasn't coming, we were so nervous that we scarcely knew what to do with ourselves.

"Looks like we're getting away with it," Adam said, in that cocksure voice of his. But he was gnawing on a hangnail, so I knew that he was still worried.

Dinner was over, and Aunt Cecile had curled up on a sofa with Jane while the two of them paged through the animal book. I don't think Aunt Cecile troubled herself to look at the pictures, not that she could have seen them very well because of her eye problems. But Jane was so content that I'm sure Aunt Cecile thought it was all worthwhile.

"What do *you* think?" I asked her.

Aunt Cecile looked up at me. "About what?" she asked.

"About maybe your brother doesn't know that Gerry left us here alone," I said.

"We aren't alone," Aunt Cecile said. "We have each other and we'll be just fine."

I glanced at Adam at the exact moment he turned to look at me. We could read each other's minds. "Let's go for a walk," I said.

"It's dark," Aunt Cecile protested, sitting up straight.

"Just down to the river," I said.

Aunt Cecile leaned back again. "Don't fall in," she said.

She amazed me. Once again she sounded like a normal . . . mother.

But when Adam and I got to the river, he said, "Doesn't she understand the trouble we're in?"

"I don't think so," I said. "She doesn't realize that we'll have to get more food and she's running out of money and we can't very well take her to the store with us because we never know when she's going to act weird again —"

"Or cry," Adam put in. "That's what I can't stand. When she cries in front of everybody."

"Ladies cry sometimes," I said, defensive and angry. "I'm talking about the crazy way she mixes up words — that aphasia. Most people don't know anything about aphasia because they've never been around anybody with a stroke — or a head injury — so they don't know that the person is really all right inside — smart, I mean. It's just that —"

"They act crazy," Adam interrupted again. "Well,

she can't go to the store and that's that. So how will we manage buying food? Did you think of that?"

He was barely visible in the dark, but I stared anyway. "You were the one who was so glad that we were left alone," I accused.

"Yeah, but I've been thinking it over."

"Do you want to phone Father Matt from town tomorrow?" I asked, scoffing.

"Are you nuts?" Adam demanded. "Of course not! We need to find a way to make this work. I don't want to starve to death."

"We won't starve," I said. But I wasn't all that certain.

I sat hugging myself to keep warm, for the wind that blew down the river from the mountains was cold and smelled of snow, even in May.

"Anything could be out here and we wouldn't know it," I said.

"Yeah," Adam said, and he sounded pleased.

"I'm going back," I said. "It's time for Jane's bath."

"Suit yourself," Adam said. "I'll stay here for a while."

I looked back once, on my way to the cabin porch, but I couldn't see him. He liked the dark! He was more a part of it than I was — I understood that much. But there was nothing else about that strange boy that made sense to me.

Aunt Cecile and Jane were both half asleep on the

sofa when I walked through the door. Aunt Cecile blinked, and I knew that for a moment she didn't remember me. But then her gray eyes grew calm again, and she said, "Did you hear the wind?"

"Yes," I said.

"It's always like that at night in spring," she said. "It's as if winter doesn't want to let go of the mountains. But in summer, when the water in the river drops even farther, you won't hear much wind. The valley is at peace then. It's wonderful."

Maybe, I thought. Probably I won't be here to see if she's right. I pulled Jane to her feet and reminded her of bath time. She was agreeable, for she liked splashing around in the water, and skipped ahead of me to get her pajamas from the bedroom.

While I ran water, Jane pulled off her dirty clothes — and I wondered about laundry. There was a washer in the closet next to the back door, but no dryer. Were there drying lines outside? I hadn't seen any, and I hadn't seen a folding rack anywhere, either.

I'd manage. If I was going to make this work, I'd have to manage dirty clothes and everything else, too.

When the tub was full, I helped Jane climb in and gave her a bar of soap I'd found in the cupboard next to the sink. There were only a dozen towels, so I'd be washing those often.

Altogether, I'd be doing more housework here than I had at the Percys'. But that was all right, if only everything else worked out. If I could turn this around so that we were some sort of family for the summer, and nothing awful happened, then maybe Jill Percy would be so impressed with how well I'd done that when autumn came she wouldn't mind if Jane and I moved back in with her.

Of course, Aunt Cecile would be well by then, and in her own apartment, and Adam — well, Adam would have run off. I didn't trust him any more than I ever had Gerry.

"My God, what happened to her!" Aunt Cecile cried from the doorway.

I'd forgotten to close the door, and now she'd seen Jane's back. Stupid me. Jane hated that. She cringed, clutching me with wet hands, nearly dragging me into the water with her.

"Don't look at her," I said to Aunt Cecile. "No one is supposed to come in when I'm giving Jane her bath."

"What happened to her back?" Aunt Cecile repeated. Her hands were shaking again, and the bad side of her face had drawn down and back as if an invisible hand had clawed at it.

"Somebody beat her with a chain," I said. I laid the wet washcloth across Jane's back to hide the scars. "Didn't Father Matt tell you?"

"He told me that she'd been — she'd been . . ."

I turned to look at Aunt Cecile.

She was wringing her hands. "He said she'd been thrown from a car on the fast — no. On the —"

"Freeway," I supplied, busying myself with Jane again so that I wouldn't have to look at Aunt Cecile's face while she struggled to find words. "Would you mind awfully much going out and closing the door? Jane gets upset when anybody else is in here."

Aunt Cecile backed out of the bathroom and shut the door. I could hear her weeping in the hall.

No, Mary Jack, I told myself, you can't make a family out of this mess. Nobody could.

I bit my lip until I was sure that I wouldn't cry, and then I said, "When you're in your pajamas, Jane, I'll read to you from the animal book. Would you like that?"

Silence. She wouldn't even look at me. She fingered the burn scars on her neck.

I slept well that night, even though I'd expected to have nightmares. In the morning, I woke before seven, and without disturbing Jane or Aunt Cecile, I dressed and crept to the kitchen.

Adam was already there, toasting a slice of bread.

"How come you're up so early?" I asked.

"Thought I'd scout around the neighborhood," he said.

"What neighborhood?" I asked as I poured water for myself and dropped another slice of bread into the old toaster. "We're the only people here."

"I want to see what's down the other path," he

said. "Tell Aunt Cecile when she gets up that I'll be back in plenty of time to chop kindling."

I glanced at him from under my eyebrows. "Seems to me that it would be easier to gather sticks from the woods."

He didn't dignify my comment with a reply. When he'd finished his dry toast and washed it down with milk, he slipped out of the cabin and disappeared down the path that led to the place where the car was parked.

He's going to run off now, I thought.

But I was wrong. Around noon, when Aunt Cecile and I were making sandwiches with the last of the bread, Adam reappeared.

I wasn't about to let him know that I'd been certain we'd never see him again. "How many neighbors did you find?" I asked.

"There are some empty cabins at a campground down the other path," he said, helping himself to a sandwich. "They're on the river, too. It curves around a point of land and widens out. I saw a place like a swimming hole."

"We can swim there," Aunt Cecile said. She frowned slightly. "But we'd better not. In summer, there are too many people. People ask questions."

"I'm not afraid of questions," Adam said.

"Only because you're a good liar," I said. He'd eaten a whole sandwich and had started on another, and we hadn't even set the table yet. But I didn't dare say anything else.

After lunch, I explained to Aunt Cecile that we would have to shop for food again. "We need almost everything," I said. "It could cost a lot. You said you can write a check?"

"Of course," she said, pushing away her plate. "I have plenty in the bank. We don't need to worry."

But I didn't like the quick fright I saw in her eyes. And I knew what scared her, too.

"You can remember how to write a check?" I asked, keeping my voice soft, careful not to hint that I thought she was mentally retarded or anything like that.

"I didn't, but I do now," she said, and she left the table, hurrying away to the bedroom. She brought back her purse.

"Here," she said, taking out a checkbook.

But when she opened it, she stopped smiling.

She put the checkbook down on the table in front of her and covered one eye with her hand.

"You're looking at the deposit slips," Adam said.

"What do you know about it?" I cried.

"I know that she's looking at the deposit slips, and you can't pay for groceries with one of those." He bent over her and flipped back to the place where the blank checks were. "Here, Aunt Cecile. These are the checks. Do you remember how to fill one out?"

She looked down at the pale pink checks, at the faint lines that didn't have instructions printed under them, and began to nod. But then she changed her mind and looked up at me.

I wasn't too certain about how to write out a check, either. "Adam, you show her," I said.

"Aw, for Pete's sake," he said, grabbing the checkbook. "See, right here? You put the date. And then you write . . ." He bent his head over the check and studied it. "You put somebody's name here. The store's! And then you write out how much money the check is going to be worth. First in numbers and then in words. And then you sign." He handed the checkbook back triumphantly.

Aunt Cecile stared down at it, dismayed. "Yes," she said. "I can see that." She covered one eye with her hand again.

I could imagine her doing that in the store. And I could imagine how the man at the store would act. We couldn't risk his refusing to accept the check, because we had to have food.

"Adam, can I talk to you for a minute outside?" I asked.

"Again?" he cried. But he followed.

"Look," I told him as soon as we reached the river, "this won't work. We can't take her to the store. She'll ruin everything."

"Well, they won't cash a check that *we* give them, especially if it's signed by somebody they don't know."

I wondered how he'd learned that, and decided that I'd better not ask. "Okay, then you think of something," I said.

He threw a rock into the river. "Maybe we can teach her to write a check before we leave."

"And then hope she doesn't freak out over something and forget?" I asked, disgusted. "That won't work."

He turned to look at me. "I could write everything on the check and then she could sign it. She ought to be able to manage her own signature."

"Wouldn't the man think it looked pretty strange?"

"We could tell him that she hurt her arm." Adam nodded, satisfied.

"But only a little bit because she can still sign her name," I said, my voice heavy with disgust. "That won't work either." I threw a couple of rocks, too, and the river swallowed them up and roared on toward Puget Sound, many miles away.

"Hey, we could tell the man that you're learning how to write checks!" Adam said. "Yeah, that would work. We could say that Aunt Cecile promised you that you could write everything but the signature. He'd buy that, because you're only a kid and kids have to learn about checks sometime."

"You do it!" I cried, furious. I was humiliated at the idea that I should be the one to have the public lesson.

"Are you nuts?" Adam demanded. "Is he going to believe that after he's seen me drive us up in the car?"

"We can't take the car!" I cried. "You don't have a license!"

"Big deal," Adam said. "You said we needed lots of food. Well, who's going to carry it?"

He was right, but that didn't make it easy. "All right," I said. "Let's go back and make sure she understands what we're going to do before we leave. We can't be fumbling around in the store, or she'll get nervous and ruin everything."

Aunt Cecile agreed with our plan, and, with Adam's help, I learned to write checks on scratch paper we found in a drawer in the kitchen.

"Now we need for you to practice your signature," Adam told Aunt Cecile. "Just to be sure everything goes smoothly."

She flushed, but she took the pencil he handed her, and wrote her name, in slow and wobbly letters, at the bottom of one of my practice checks.

Adam rolled his eyes and glared at me, as if her writing were all my fault.

"Do it a few more times," he said, and Aunt Cecile obeyed.

Jane nudged me and presented me with a drawing.

I was tempted to send her away because we were busy, but the laughter in her eyes stopped me.

She'd drawn three people standing around a very tall table (Jane wasn't good at drawing people sitting down) and writing on sheets of paper. All the people were scowling.

"Jane thinks we're jerks," I said, showing the others her drawing.

Adam glared at the figures on the paper. "Jeez, *she* should talk," he said. "Come on, everybody, let's try one more practice check, just to make sure we know what we're doing."

And so I wrote out a check to "Monarch River Groceries" for fifty-eight dollars and forty cents. Aunt Cecile added her signature, shaky but legible. The three of us burst out laughing.

"Monarch River, here we come," Adam said.

We were back in two hours, with enough food to last for quite a while, but the check had been for nearly two hundred dollars. However, we'd succeeded in everything, even convincing the man in the store that "Mama" had promised me I could make out the check before she signed it. The man, pleased with what I'd done, rewarded me with a gap-toothed smile and told me I was a smart girl. He didn't know that Adam was nudging my ankle with his dirty sneaker.

And he didn't ask who had driven the car from the river to the town. He hadn't even seen the car, since

Adam had parked out of sight around the side of the store.

At the end of the road, Adam and I made three trips between the car and the cabin before we had all the food carried in. We had fried chicken for dinner, chocolate cake for dessert, and went to bed early.

That night the rains began, and it rained all the rest of the week. But we had food and firewood, and the main room bookcases were full of books.

With every day that passed, we were more certain that Gerry hadn't bothered telling Father Matt that we were alone. But every day brought us closer to Saturday, when he would come to see us and discover that we'd been living there on our own.

"He'll be pleased," Aunt Cecile said when I told her I was worried.

"He'll take us back to town," I confided in Adam.

"I'm not going back," he said. "No way."

Thunder rolled all Friday night, but that wasn't why I lay awake in my bunk. I was certain that this was my last night at the cabin, and my last chance to have a family. I was much too old to adopt now.

Around midnight, I began biting my nails again.

❧ CHAPTER 7 ❧

We were prepared for Father Matt's visit by ten on Saturday morning. The cabin was shining clean, and Adam not only had built a fire to warm the damp main room, but had also invented a story to account for Gerry's absence.

"If he believes that she's still here, he won't even think about taking us back," Adam explained when I expressed my doubts.

"What about next week, when he comes back?" I asked. "And the week after that?"

"I can think up a different story for every Saturday all summer long," Adam said. He meant "lie," not "story," and if I'd had his experience in making up tall tales, I'd have shut up about it instead of bragging.

Aunt Cecile was so nervous that she paced from the fireplace, across the length of the main room, and down the hall to the bedrooms, over and over. Jane, sucking her thumb furiously, had tried to crawl under

80

the lower bunks, but the spaces were blocked with storage boxes. Finally, out of desperation, she crawled behind a sofa and flattened herself against the wall. I left her there, since she seemed happy enough once she was out of sight.

At twenty after ten, Father Matt, dressed in his clerical black, climbed the steps to the porch and threw open the door. He carried a portable TV in one hand and magazines in the other.

"Here I am, everybody!" he called out, as if we weren't all in the main room, gawking at him. He'd forgotten his raincoat, and so he was wet from the light rain.

"Matt!" Aunt Cecile said, sounding startled, as if she had been caught at something.

"Hi," Adam said, his voice gruff. I was extremely pleased that he was nervous. A person ought to be, if he planned to tell an enormous lie within the next couple of minutes.

"Father Matt," I said. "Nice to see you. Too bad it's still raining." I was chattering a little too fast, but I knew he wouldn't notice. He never did.

No, I think he did notice when people were up to something. But he didn't know what to do about liars, cheats, thieves, or whiners like his wife, so he pretended that he didn't see or hear anything that made people look less than perfect.

"Where's Jane?" Father Matt asked. "Where's my Janie girl?"

"Behind the sofa," I said, pointing.

He got down on his knees and peered underneath. "I see a foot and an arm and some pretty blond hair," he said. "Do you suppose that a fairy princess is hiding behind the sofa?"

Jane crept out, to stare at him, dark eyes unblinking. I thought I saw one corner of her mouth quirk in what might have been a smile. But with her, there was no telling.

Father Matt picked her up and put her on the sofa next to him. "Now, people, tell me everything you've been doing."

Adam and I did most of the talking, quickly, because Aunt Cecile was coming to pieces and I didn't want her to try saying anything and end up bawling. I suppose Adam was worried about the same thing.

We told Father Matt about the rain and the ducks on the pond and the eagle. And how Adam cut kindling every day for our fires. And how much we were all eating.

That was a mistake.

Father Matt said, "Speaking of eating, where's Gerry?"

Adam burst out laughing and then sobered abruptly when he realized that Father Matt hadn't been making fun of Gerry's weight, but instead was thinking of her as the family cook.

Father Matt looked around, flushed and miserable.

"Oh, dear," he said. "I only meant that she's been fixing your meals."

"You bet," Adam said. "And she's a *good* cook, too." It was clear that he was feeling comfortable with lying. Not that I was surprised.

"Gerry's a good cook?" Father Matt asked, astonished. "Well, ah, fine. Do you suppose she'd fix me a cup of coffee?"

"She's not here," I blurted, and Adam said the same thing at the same time. He scowled at me.

"She's gone off shopping somewhere with a friend," Adam said.

"A friend? She knows someone here in Monarch River?" Father Matt looked at Aunt Cecile for an answer.

"She ran into someone when she was grocery shopping," Adam said. "They hadn't seen each other for a long time."

"But the station wagon is parked at the turnaround," Father Matt said, bewildered. "She surely didn't walk in this rain."

"The friend picked her up," Adam said.

"Yes," Aunt Cecile said. "Betty somebody-or-other."

We'd rehearsed a name, but Aunt Cecile didn't remember it. Oh well, I told myself. Anybody could make a mistake like that.

Father Matt seemed relieved. "I worried that

Gerry might not have a good time here."

"She doesn't seem to mind too much," I said.

Adam and I had had a long argument earlier that morning about whether or not we ought to say that Gerry didn't mind being here. Adam was all for telling Father Matt that Gerry liked the cabin, but I knew Gerry better than he did, and I assured him that nobody would believe that she liked it there. Not even Father Matt, who would believe almost anything.

Aunt Cecile backed me up. "No, Gerry hasn't complained too much," she said. She smiled, and I was surprised to see that her smile wasn't as crooked as it usually was.

Father Matt noticed that, too. "I do believe that you're feeling a little better, Cecile."

She nodded. "Coffee," she said. "We'll make coffee." She gestured to me and I followed her to the kitchen.

I wasn't too sure she and I could manage coffee. I'd never made it, and she could use only one hand. And she got things in the kitchen mixed up sometimes. The night before she'd poured the last of our milk down the sink instead of into our glasses. That morning Jane had powdered milk instead, with chocolate flavoring.

Between the two of us, with lots of whispered questions, we filled the electric pot with water and coffee and plugged it in.

"Coffee will be ready soon," I said as I stuck my head through the kitchen doorway. I could only hope I was right, and that the pot wouldn't explode instead.

Father Matt and Adam were sitting across the coffee table from one another, and Adam was telling lies about how Aunt Cecile taught us to play Monopoly. *I* taught Adam and Aunt Cecile, and neither of them was very good at it — Adam because he didn't care and Aunt Cecile because she couldn't remember anything or count.

"She's getting better, all right," Father Matt told Adam. "I knew she would when she got up here, her favorite place in the whole world. I was always surprised that she and David didn't move up here after our parents died. I suppose it was too far for David to commute to work. And Cecile wouldn't find many piano students in Monarch River. Of course, she could always teach in the school. I've heard that they have a hard time finding teachers."

"She's a teacher?" Adam asked. He hated teachers, and I wondered if now he'd lose his newfound respect for Aunt Cecile.

"Oh, my, yes," Father Matt said. "One of the best. But she left teaching years ago and concentrated on her music."

"Smart," Adam said. "Music is better than school."

I stopped eavesdropping. The conversation seemed to be going all right.

Aunt Cecile was looking out the window over the sink. "The rain's dried," she said.

"Stopped," I corrected automatically. And then I stared at her. She'd better not make a mistake like that where her brother could hear her. "How are you feeling? Will you be able to hang on until he goes?"

She bit her lip, then said, "I must, for all our sakes."

I nodded. I understood that sort of attitude. But I was afraid that she'd fall apart, once Father Matt left — if we pulled off our scheme and he left without us, that is.

The coffeepot quit rumbling and gushing, so I guessed that the coffee was done and took two mugs out of the cupboard. I filled both of them, put them on a tray with a plate of cookies, and carried the tray into the main room.

"Coffee is served," I said.

Aunt Cecile came in and sat close to the coffee table. I put her cup in front of her and then served Father Matt.

"You've become a fine hostess," Father Matt said to me.

I panicked. Had he guessed that I'd taken over most of the cooking and serving?

"Not really," I babbled. "But Aunt Cecile is teaching me."

Father Matt looked up from the plate of cookies. "You call her Aunt Cecile? Wonderful. I'm so glad to hear that. I'm sure Jill will be glad to know that we're all one big family."

"Sure," Adam said, and he snorted. But when Father Matt turned toward him, Adam smiled and looked as innocent as Jane.

We asked him lots of questions, as we'd planned, about what was going on in the parish and Jill's school, and how the roses were coming along. Father Matt went on and on about the garden, while I waited, screwing up my courage, to ask the big question, the one Adam and I had fought over because we were both so anxious to avoid it. But it had to be asked.

"What does Mrs. Frank think about our spending the summer here?" I asked. "You did tell her, didn't you?"

There was danger here. If Mrs. Frank didn't like the idea, we could be hauled back to town no matter how successfully we seemed to be getting along.

Father Matt fiddled with a cookie, nibbled it, and put it down on the table. "As a matter of fact, children, I haven't mentioned it to her yet. I've been so busy . . . well, yes. Busy. And I don't expect her to be in touch with us again until late August. By then you may be back in town. Or perhaps not yet. In any event, we'll cross that bridge when we come to it."

In other words, he was scared to death of Mrs.

Frank and didn't want to do anything that might attract attention to us.

Adam and I exchanged a glance. I couldn't read his expression, but I hoped he read mine. Leave it alone, I told him in my mind. *Leave it alone.*

"Would you like more coffee?" Aunt Cecile asked.

"No, sister, I've got to be going," he said. "I wish I could spend the day with you, but I have a wedding at four, and I must get back."

He got to his feet and picked up Jane for a last hug. I was so relieved that I had spots in front of my eyes. We were going to get away with it!

"Uh, hey," Adam began. He gnawed fiercely at a hangnail. "Gerry said that if you left before she got back, we were to remind you about the grocery money for next week."

"Of course!" Father Matt cried. "How stupid of me! I nearly left without giving it to you, and then what would you have done?" He pulled out his wallet and handed Aunt Cecile several twenty-dollar bills. "Did you have enough this last week?"

"Yes," Aunt Cecile said, just as Adam began speaking. "I know this is hard for you, Matt, and I hope you know how much I appreciate it. I'll make it up to you and Jill, when I'm . . ."

Oh, no, she was turning pale and starting to shake. That was too long a speech for her to make, and she'd been upset anyway.

"It was exactly enough money," I said quickly, and

I grabbed Father Matt's hand. "Can we walk back to the car with you?"

"In the rain?" he said, distracted from his sister. "Of course not." He tucked my hand under his arm and led me to the door. "The weather should change for the better this afternoon," he said. "I'll bet you children will be glad about that."

"Yes," I said.

Adam had opened the door. We all, except for Jane, walked out on the porch. Aunt Cecile looked as if she was ready to cry.

"It's time for Jane's nap," I said, desperate for an excuse to get rid of Father Matt. "She's been taking naps since we got here. Aunt Cecile says it's good for her."

"Yes, yes," Father Matt said. "Naps are good. Goodbye and God bless, dear ones. I'll see you next Saturday. Give my regards to Gerry and tell her I'm sorry I missed her."

"Will do," Adam said. "See you next week."

Father Matt ducked his head and ran through the rain toward the path.

"We did it," Adam said.

We filed back in the house and I closed the door.

"We're safe for another week," I told Aunt Cecile. "And we've got cash for food, too."

"Let's have lunch," she said, "then go into town for a treat."

"It's still raining," I said.

"Adam will drive," she said. "For now. Pretty soon I'll be driving again, and then we'll go all the way to Snohomish, or some place like that. We'll go everywhere!"

She didn't notice Adam's face. I wasn't too sure that he wanted her well enough to drive.

"Adam, give Aunt Cecile the money to keep," I said.

He handed it over willingly, but afterward, while I was making sandwiches in the kitchen, he came in and said, "You thought I was going to keep the money, didn't you? Well, I'm not like Gerry."

"I didn't say you were," I said.

"You were thinking it," he accused. He left the kitchen and went to his bedroom.

He was right. I had been thinking it. I knew that with a handful of money and a car, Adam could go a long way before anyone knew he was gone.

So let him, I told myself. What do I care?

But I knew that I wouldn't be able to cover up his disappearance as well as I had Gerry's. And if Father Matt ever figured out what happened, he wouldn't be able to pretend anymore that everything here was all right.

❧ CHAPTER 8 ❧

Blazing summer arrived suddenly in Monarch River, catching us by surprise. The hot sun shone for the entire week after Father Matt's visit, and the woods became the setting for a fairy tale. Wildflowers bloomed everywhere. Twice in those first sunny days, we saw deer within twenty feet of the cabin. And shy Jane made friends with a young raccoon that followed her to the porch.

"You must never touch him, though," Aunt Cecile told Jane. "He might bite."

Jane's dark eyes blinked once, accepting this rule, and then she went back to tearing up bits of bread for her alert friend.

I washed clothes that week — none of us had anything clean left to wear — and Aunt Cecile dug out a pair of old pulleys and a long loop of rope.

"A clothesline," she said. She smiled suddenly. "Hey, I said that word right!"

"You say lots of words right," I said.

"But not hard ones like *clothesline*," she said. "I must be getting better."

I didn't argue. If she thought saying *clothesline* right made up for calling the television set the elevator every time she talked about it, then who was I to criticize? Anyway, Adam was listening to this conversation, and if I'd said one thing to Aunt Cecile that implied she was less than perfect, he'd have had a fit. She was the only one he liked.

Adam helped put up the clothesline, first climbing up a cedar tree near the porch to tie on one of the pulleys and string the rope. Then he climbed the second cedar Aunt Cecile pointed out, looped the rope around the other pulley, and tied it on the trunk.

"Looks pretty good to me," he said.

"The rope should be tighter," Aunt Cecile said. "Or higher. Something's wrong. It didn't hang this close to the ground when my father did it."

"It's high enough," Adam said, and he nodded his head.

But Aunt Cecile was right. I'd barely begun hanging out the wet clothes when we could see that much more weight would pull the rope down so far that the clothes would drag in the dirt.

Aunt Cecile persuaded Adam to move one of the pulleys higher. "But you have to take down the clothes first," he said, "or the line will be too heavy."

Aunt Cecile reached out to grab Jane's pajamas and missed them. I saw her squint one eye shut and try again. That time she got hold of the cloth.

"Why can you see better with one eye closed?" I asked.

"I never did understand exactly what double vision is all about," she said. "I only know that I've got it and it drives me crazy." She pulled one of Adam's T-shirts off the line and dropped it in the basket on top of Jane's pajamas.

"Will it go away?" I asked.

"Yes," she said. "At least, that's what the doctors said, but sometimes I think they only told me things like that to keep me from worrying. Or to stop me from complaining."

I couldn't imagine what it would be like to see two edges of everything where I should see only one. That alone would have driven me crazy. But to have all of Aunt Cecile's other problems — language and reading and writing and remembering, as well as the weak arm — would have been unbearable.

Adam climbed the tree again and moved the pulley higher, until it seemed that our clothes might be flapping above the cabin roof.

"That's good!" Aunt Cecile called out.

She tried to hang up the things she'd taken down, but that wasn't so easy, and she fumbled so much that I took over. By the time Adam reached the porch again, I'd hung up half the clothes. The next load was waiting in the washer.

Jane produced a sketch to celebrate the clothesline. She drew the line stretching nearly straight up into the sky, with stiff clothes sticking out from it. She showed Aunt Cecile with only one eye. And she showed me scowling.

It took me a while to find Adam in her drawing, and then I saw that she'd colored him green, like the tree.

"This is wonderful," I told her. "But you still don't draw yourself. Won't you put Jane in this picture?"

She took the drawing back and went in the cabin without looking back.

"Why doesn't she draw herself?" I asked Aunt Cecile.

Aunt Cecile looked after Jane, and then said, "I suppose she draws what she sees, like taking a snapshot with a camera, and naturally she wouldn't be in her own snapshot."

That sounded logical and grown-up — but it didn't sound *right*. I could remember drawing pictures when I was a little kid, and I always put myself in them.

"How long does it take clothes to dry?" Adam asked. "What if everything is still wet tomorrow?"

"Everything will be dry this afternoon," Aunt Cecile said. "Wait and see."

She was right. By four o'clock, we had clean, dry clothes. And they smelled like the outdoors. Even Adam noticed.

Father Matt came at ten o'clock the next Saturday, and Adam lied to him, saying that he'd just missed Gerry by five minutes — she'd gone into town to have her hair cut.

Father Matt didn't mind. He'd brought oatmeal cookies that one of his parishioners had made for us, and so we feasted while we sat on the riverbank and watched the eagle overhead. He left before eleven o'clock, satisfied once again that we were doing well.

When he was out of sight, Adam produced the money Father Matt had left for Gerry. "We're still in business," he said.

"I feel guilty, lying to him about Gerry," I said.

"Not me," Adam said. "You gotta do what you gotta do."

He was right, of course. But I was having a hard time with what I had to do.

On the following Saturday, Adam hid the station wagon partway down an old logging road. Father Matt arrived on time, with a crate of strawberries, magazines for Gerry, and a note from Crystal, one of my school friends, telling me that she missed me.

"When I saw that the car was gone, I was afraid

none of you would be here," he said. "Gerry's taken off somewhere, has she?"

"She drove her friend to the doctor," Adam said.

"Oh, that's a shame," Father Matt said. "I hope it was nothing serious."

"She sprained her wrist," Adam lied, smooth as whipped cream.

"Tell Gerry I'm sorry I missed her again," Father Matt said.

After he left, and I had a moment alone with Adam, I said, "I can't believe that Father Matt falls for your lies every week."

"Not everybody would," Adam admitted. "But the priest will keep right on doing it."

"But why?" I asked, horrified. I felt so bad, taking advantage of Father Matt that way, but I couldn't think of anything else to do.

"Believing lies is easier than noticing that something might be wrong that you'd have to fix," Adam said. "That's how grown-ups are sometimes. They take the quick and easy way out."

"That's crazy!" I cried. "You are really rotten, you know that?"

"Sure," Adam said, grinning. "Who cares?"

Nobody, I thought. And that was even more terrible.

Our peace ended that weekend. The summer people arrived at the campground down the other path, and the woods rang with shouts and laughter. Adam and I sneaked down the path to spy on them, then returned to report to Aunt Cecile.

"There are three families with little kids about Jane's age," I said.

Adam nodded, and said, "And one couple, a man and a woman, with a big TV. They've got it outside on the porch, so everybody can see it and be jealous, I guess. But it doesn't work right because the antenna isn't high enough, so he's trying to rig up something better on his roof."

"I hope no one comes here," Aunt Cecile said, and she sounded worried. "I don't want to question any sharpings."

"Answer any questions," I corrected. "No, we don't want anybody snooping around."

"I'll run 'em off," Adam boasted.

"No, don't do that," Aunt Cecile said, and she was wringing her hands.

"That would make them suspicious," I said.

Adam understood. "Well, what shall we do, then?"

But we weren't going to get help from Aunt Cecile, because she'd lost what little confidence she'd built up. She paced the floor and finally wept.

"It won't work," she said. "They'll catch us and send us back. Jill's there, so bad, I can't stand it, no."

"Aw, jeez," Adam groaned. He took her arm and

led her to the sofa. "Sit down and rest. Do you want a cup of tea? Mary Jack can fix it."

"I'll get it right now," I said, hurrying toward the kitchen. Sometimes we could head off Aunt Cecile's bad times with a cup of tea and a little talk about the ducks on the pond or the eagle.

Jane pattered after me, clutching the hem of my shirt.

"What do you want?" I asked, impatient with her.

But she didn't answer. She only looked at me.

"Don't be scared," I said, and I knelt beside her and put my arms around her. "Auntie's only a little tired. Things aren't going to get bad again."

I hoped I was right.

Later that afternoon, we had a visitor. A man appeared on our porch while I was slicing tomatoes for our salad. He rapped on the open door and yelled, "Anybody home?"

Aunt Cecile had been helping Jane change out of her wet clothes — she'd gone wading in a shallow river pool with Adam — and when she heard the knocking, she ran to the main room, her face pale.

"Hello, missus," the man said, extending his hand to shake hers. "I'm Don Snyder. The wife and I rented one of the cabins east of here."

"How do you do," Aunt Cecile said. She didn't

smile at the rat-faced man, and she withdrew her hand from his. "I am Mrs. Bradshaw."

The man's smile faltered. "Thought I'd make your acquaintance. Is Mr. Bradshaw around?"

"He's dead," Aunt Cecile said, her voice chilly.

"Sorry!" Don Snyder blurted. "Well, say, I don't want to bother you, but . . ." He saw Adam then and stuck out his hand again. "How do you do, son. What's your name?"

"Adam," Adam growled, and he put his hand in his pocket. "You want something?"

Adam startled the man, and for a moment he was silent. Then he cleared his throat and said, "I wondered if you folks have a few tools I could borrow. I need wire cutters, a hammer . . ."

"No machines," Aunt Cecile said. "No . . ."

My heart sank to my feet. She meant no tools, but her aphasia had caught up with her again, and she realized it, too, because her lips trembled.

"We don't have any tools," Adam said, his voice too loud. "We did have some, but one of the summer people stole them out of our shed." He looked accusingly at Don Snyder.

"Hey," the man protested. He backed up a step. "Okay then, I guess I'll have to ask around."

"Why don't you borrow from the other people at the campground?" I asked. "They're closer to you than we are."

His face flushed. "Yeah, well . . ."

He came here to snoop, to see what we were like, I thought. He didn't even try to borrow tools from the other summer people.

"Anything else?" Adam demanded.

The man looked around. "Guess I interrupted something," he said. He stared hard at Aunt Cecile. "Are you okay, missus?"

"Goodbye," Aunt Cecile said. Her voice was weak and shaky.

The man was unable to hide his curiosity. "Strange place, for a woman and her kids, all alone like this."

"We have lots of relatives that come here to stay," I said.

"If it's any of your business," Adam added.

The man stared frankly at Aunt Cecile now. "What's wrong with you? You sick or something?"

She didn't answer him. Jane, who had been sitting on the sofa with her animal book, pretending that he wasn't there, suddenly jumped up and scuttled down the hall toward the bedroom.

"Shouldn't you be looking for a place to get the tools you need?" Adam asked.

"Yes, you bet," the man said, and he backed to the door, smiling at Aunt Cecile. "See you again, Missus . . . Bradshaw, was it? Yes, Bradshaw. See you again real soon. And you take care."

He'd disappeared down the path before any of us spoke.

"He's trouble," Adam said.

"No, he's not," I said. "He won't come back."

"Sure he will," Adam said. "He's curious about us. He'll be back soon, and make trouble just for the fun of it."

Aunt Cecile sat down in a chair abruptly, as if her legs were about to give out. "My fault," she said. "I'm so sorry."

"We can handle it," I said. "What harm can he do?"

But I knew the answer. Aunt Cecile had acted loony, Jane had run off like a scared cat, and Adam had been rude. You didn't have to be smart to see that lots of people would be curious about a family that seemed so anxious to get rid of a neighbor.

He was the exact opposite of Father Matt. And neither one of them was particularly safe, but for very different reasons.

❧ CHAPTER 9 ❧

For the next couple of days, Aunt Cecile was quiet and withdrawn. She seldom spoke, even during mealtimes, and she spent hours alone by the pond, watching the fish and baby ducks.

"One of these days I'll walk out there and find that the blackberry vines have grown over her," Adam said one afternoon after he'd come back from the pond.

"Thanks for checking up on her," I said. I grew more worried every day. Aunt Cecile had counted on recovering during the summer, but the arrival of the summer people had set her back.

"We'd better think of a way of hiding her next Saturday when the priest comes," Adam said. "He'll know she's worse. It's so bad he can't ignore it."

I stared at him. "What are we supposed to do with her? Lock her up in the shed?"

Adam stared back. "No, rocks-for-brains! I'll drive her somewhere and you can tell the priest that she and

Gerry went off shopping for clothes or something."

"And what am I supposed to tell him about you?" I demanded.

"Tell him I'm fishing up the river somewhere."

"I hate this lying!" I shouted. "I'm terrible at it."

"The priest won't care," Adam said. "As long as we keep his sister out of sight, he won't look around for trouble."

I'm ashamed to say that Adam was right. On the following Saturday, he told Aunt Cecile that he wanted to practice driving, and he asked her to go along so that if he got stopped he'd have a licensed driver in the car and wouldn't get into trouble.

Jane and I cleaned the main room until it gleamed, then sat and waited for Father Matt. He came, carrying pastry and magazines, and left, believing all my lies. I felt sick with guilt.

Adam and Aunt Cecile returned an hour and a half later. I'd expected her to be upset, because she hated riding in cars so much, and they'd been gone a long time. But she was smiling and acted as if she felt much better.

"Where did you guys go?" I asked.

"I showed Adam how to get to the horse farm," she said. "We stayed and talked to Al Stewart for a while, and then looked at the new colts." Adam was grinning and nodding behind her.

"Everything went all right then?" I asked.

"You mean about Adam's driving?" Aunt Cecile

asked. "Oh, he's a fine driver. But I can't understand how he got that way, being so young." She bustled off toward the bedroom then, leaving me open-mouthed behind her.

"What happened?" I whispered to Adam.

He laughed aloud. "It was great, really great. This old guy — well, he's her age, so he's only a little bit old — he came running around the side of the house looking like he'd won a million dollars. He yells, 'Cecile, is it you? Is it really you?' "

"How did she handle it?" I demanded.

"Fine. He acts crazy about her, and he practically bawled when she told him that her husband was dead. But, boy, she sure perked up when he took us around to this big field to see the mares and colts." Adam scratched his elbow and looked thoughtful for a moment. "Al's not a bad guy. She's invited him to come for dinner tomorrow night."

"She asked a stranger to come here for dinner?" I exclaimed. "You let her?"

"He's not a stranger!" Adam insisted. "She knew him years ago, when she was in high school. He's okay. He won't make trouble."

But I wasn't too sure.

The next morning we went to town to shop for the special dinner. Aunt Cecile actually wrote out a list. It was weird — she wrote "potatoters" instead of "potatoes" — but it was a real list, more than she'd ever been able to manage before. And when we got to the store, she even talked to the man behind the counter for a couple of minutes before we collected the groceries we needed.

She and I spent most of the afternoon in the kitchen, cooking potatoes for salad and frying chicken. It wasn't until an hour before the man was supposed to arrive that she slipped out of focus again.

"I don't think I can handle this," she said, after she'd dropped the mayonnaise jar on the floor, breaking it.

"We've got another jar," I said. "Don't work yourself into a state. Go sit down while I clean this up and I'll fix you some tea in a minute."

"I'm the grown-up. You shouldn't be taking care of me."

I looked up from where I was kneeling, cleaning up the mess. "You can have a turn being the grown-up when that man gets here," I said. "Right now, I have to do it."

I didn't dare let her know how angry I was about the man. Who cared that he was an old friend? She was putting everything at risk. What if she had one of her bad spells when he was here? What if he took it into his head to phone Father Matt and ask why he let his sick sister stay in a cabin with only three children for company? It wouldn't take much for Father Matt to sort out what was going on.

No, not even if Adam was right and Father Matt didn't really want to know whether or not Gerry was still around. Just a stranger knowing about our trouble would cause Father Matt to do something.

It was important that this Al think that Aunt Cecile was her old self. And for that to happen, she had to calm down. I fixed a whole pot of tea for her.

When I carried the tea into the main room, I found that Jane was with Aunt Cecile, patiently standing before her with one of her drawings. But Aunt Cecile's eyes were closed, shutting out the world.

"Aunt Cecile," I said, making my voice light and cheerful even though I could have screamed. "Jane's brought you a wonderful drawing." I glanced quickly at the paper. "A wonderful picture of the ducks at the pond."

Well, I hoped that those creatures were ducks. Jane drew people better than she drew birds and animals.

Aunt Cecile opened her eyes and reached for the paper. "Lovely, Jane," she said. The paper shook in her hand.

"Here's tea," I said, before she began apologizing for her trembling hand, her failures, her illness, her life. "Drink it up and then why don't you change into that pink blouse and put your hair up the way Adam likes?"

Aunt Cecile smiled — and I saw with relief that the smile was straight, not crooked. Maybe she was feeling better.

"My hair," she began, hesitating. My heart sank.

"You don't have to put it up," I said.

"My hair," she repeated, and that time her smile jerked. "It's a mess, I know. But I'm so otherwise — no. I'm so . . ."

"Tired," I finished.

"No!" she said, her voice sharp.

I nearly dropped the teapot. Now what?

"I'm not tired, I'm *nervous*," she said. She reached out and touched my hand. "Sorry, sorry. I'm crabby, too."

"Don't apologize," I said. I would have gone back to the kitchen to finish the potato salad, but I had to say something else. "Aunt Cecile, no matter what, don't tell your friend you're sorry about anything, okay? It sounds like . . . well, it sounds like something's wrong, and we don't want him to think that. He might call your brother."

She turned her face toward me, stricken.

I raised my hand in protest. "Now don't get scared," I babbled. "But I had to say that. You just think about it a little and you'll see that it's important that your friend doesn't have a reason to call Father Matt. Okay?"

"Oh, God, what did I do?" she cried. "I shouldn't have asked him to come here."

"It's fine to have company," I said. "But we need to be careful — and not let him stay too long."

I went back to the salad then, thinking hard. I

needed Adam to help ensure that the man didn't stay long, but his usual way of clearing a room — by insulting everybody in it — wouldn't do.

When Adam came in with a load of freshly split kindling for the after-dinner fire, I called him into the kitchen and explained the problem.

"You're right," he said, surprising me. "Al's nice, but he's got to go home as soon as we finish eating."

"Not that soon!" I said. "He's got to have his dessert and coffee first, so that everything looks right."

"Okay, then as soon as I light the fire, I'll say, 'Aunt Cecile, is your headache better?' Then he'll leave so she can rest."

"Don't say headache!" I cried. "He'll want to know how she got it and if she starts talking about the accident . . ."

"Or worse, if she forgets again that she had one . . ."

"This is going to be a disaster," I said.

"No, it won't. We just have to think up something he'll believe. I know. We'll blame it on Jane. She acts like a freak anyway —"

"She does not!"

"Don't argue now!" he shouted. "She does too act like a freak, so we'll say that she's had a bad day and needs her quiet time."

"Aunt Cecile ought to be the one to say that," I said. "We'll sound like we're the ones doing all the bossing if we say it."

Adam sagged against the counter. "Okay, then what?"

I sliced olives on the cutting board. "How about if we start yawning and tell him we all go to bed early?"

"*That* early? It won't even be dark yet."

"We're kids. What does an old bachelor know about kids?" I scraped the olives over the salad.

Adam snickered. "About as much as anybody else," he said. "Okay, we'll yawn. Can you get Jane to do it?"

"She does it anyway," I said.

Al Stewart came exactly on time, carrying flowers for Aunt Cecile and jellybeans for us.

Aunt Cecile invited him in. He was so tall, taller even than Father Matt, that he had to duck his head coming through the door. He didn't have much hair, and what there was of it was gray. His face was nice and lean, his eyes were dark blue, his nose was long, and his skin tanned dark as leather.

But he was shy. "How do you do, children?" he said to Jane and me. Then he added, "I mean, girls." And then he added, "I guess I should have said young ladies."

He needed help with the knots in his conversation, so I said, "Jane and I are fine. Adam's washing up. We'll be ready to eat in a couple of minutes." And I marched off to the kitchen to let him see how busy I was, but I watched him from the door.

Aunt Cecile invited him to sit down. He chose a chair near the fireplace. Jane watched him suspiciously for a moment, then took her animal book out to the porch.

"Jane doesn't speak," Aunt Cecile said. "We don't know if she can or not. And she's not very comfortable with people she doesn't know."

Al looked after Jane. "She's your brother's foster child or yours?" he asked.

Oh, no. How would Aunt Cecile handle a question that complicated?

"We share," she said.

It was a silly answer, but Al didn't seem to be worried about it. Adam came in then, with his hair combed for a change, wearing a clean shirt. He shook hands with Al, sat down across from him, and immediately began a conversation about horses that lasted until I had the table set.

"Dinner's ready," I said.

As planned, Adam rushed everybody to the table, even yanking Jane in from the porch. Ordinarily his touch would have sent her scrambling for the bedroom, but this time she merely pulled her arm free, gave him a look as mean as a slap, and took her place at the table.

The meal went better than I could have expected. Al didn't appear to notice that Aunt Cecile had only one good hand, and she didn't eat much, which left fewer chances for an accident. Jane managed everything without a spill, too. After a while I quit worrying and ate a little myself.

Al had a big appetite. He praised the food over and over, and I had to remind Aunt Cecile with a nudge of my foot not to confess that I had fixed most of the meal.

"Aunt Cecile is a great cook," Adam said. "We're all going to get fat."

"Come over to the ranch and I'll work it off you," Al said.

I could tell by the light in Adam's eyes that he would have loved spending his days on the ranch, so I didn't give him a chance to accept. "Adam," I said, "will you bring in the cake?"

He shot me an angry look, but he did as I asked. Then, as soon as we'd finished our dessert, I interrupted a conversation about a mare who'd had an undersized colt to ask Adam to build the fire.

"It gets pretty cold here in the evenings," I told Al, "so we like to warm the cabin up just before we go to bed."

If he'd been tempted to remark that the sun was still above the horizon, he didn't. While Adam built the fire — a small one — we stepped out on the porch together.

"We're so glad you came for dinner," I said.

"You're a regular little housewife, aren't you?" Al said, smiling down at me.

"She's a valuable help to me," Aunt Cecile said,

right on cue. She put her good hand on my shoulder and only she and I knew that it was trembling slightly.

We watched Al walk along the path until he was out of sight, and then we shut ourselves inside.

"We did it," Adam said.

"It was all lovely," Aunt Cecile said. "We must ask him here again sometime." Then she noticed my horrified expression and added, "But not too soon."

Later, when she and I were alone in the kitchen, I said, "You're better again, aren't you?"

She nodded. "I was afraid this afternoon, but everything turned out all right. I was right to ask him here. He was always a gentle man, like his horses. Shy and gentle. *He* won't hurt us."

I thought that was the strangest thing to say. *He* won't hurt us? But late that night I figured it out. She was remembering our new neighbor, Don Snyder.

People like Aunt Cecile and Jane can read the inner workings of people's minds much better than the rest of us can. Those two — so fragile and hurt — knew everything about danger.

CHAPTER 10

Sometimes I was desperate to be alone. I couldn't remember how long it had been since I wasn't responsible for taking care of somebody. And I couldn't remember when there wasn't cleaning or washing or cooking waiting for me. Usually I didn't mind. No, that's not true. I didn't dare resent it. But sometimes I wanted to be a little kid, free to sit in the woods alone. Magic time.

On Friday morning, after I made sure that Aunt Cecile had a grip on herself, I left her and Jane together and walked to the road by myself. I had no idea where Adam was, and I didn't care. He'd taken to creeping off and coming back when it suited him. I cared only that he returned, not because I liked him, but because he could cause Jane and me too much trouble if he ran away.

The path that wound beside the pond was hard to find now, because the rich summer undergrowth had spread to hide it. Even though we walked there nearly every day, our feet didn't wear the trail bare. But the path that led to the right from where the road ended was as clear as it had been in May because so many people used it. Sometimes there were four cars besides ours parked there.

I was tempted to turn down the path toward the campground and see what was going on. But there was too much risk of being seen. So instead, I headed back toward our cabin.

I was halfway home when I heard rustling in the heavy brush. Just as I turned my head, I caught a glimpse of a dull gold, clumsy body. A dog?

"Hey!" I called out. "Come here, pup. Come here."

Brush crackled. I followed, pushing my way through a tangle of huckleberries. "Come here, dog."

I passed a great, upturned tree stump, and almost missed the flash of anxious brown eyes. A frightened dog peered up at me from the hollow under the heavy roots.

I knelt on the moss. "Don't be scared." The dog drew back, trembling. When I reached out my hand, it flinched.

"Aw," I groaned. "You're scared. I won't hurt you. Come on, doggie. Come see Mary Jack."

The dog cringed and turned its head, afraid to look at me.

I stretched out on my stomach and reached as far as I could, barely touching the dog's rough coat. "I'm a

114

friend," I crooned. "I like dogs, especially pretty yellow ones. Come on, look at me."

I lay there talking for a long time, my arm stretched out so far that my shoulder hurt. Finally the dog turned its dark eyes toward me and its tail flapped a couple of times.

"That's it," I said. "You come on out and say hello."

The dog inched out, the whites of its eyes showing. But it wouldn't get to its feet. Instead, it crawled to me, humble and worried. Then I saw that it was a female, and expecting puppies.

That broke my heart. I was sure she was a stray, for she wore no collar and she was horribly thin. How could she raise a family out here in the woods? Where was she getting food?

"You'd better come home with me," I said, and I stood up. "Come on, lady." I snapped my fingers — and she cringed.

I knelt beside her again, fondling her ears. "Come home with me and we'll take care of you."

But she scuttled back down under the roots again, exactly as Jane would have done.

I needed help with her. I started home, crashing through the brush instead of using the path, not caring how brambles ripped at my jeans and snagged my hair. I passed the pond, out of breath, and I didn't even glance at the baby ducks. A crow squawked at me, protesting my passage.

The cabin was in sight. And so was Jane. She was coming up the narrow trail from the river, followed by the raccoon she fed every day. And both of them were followed by Don Snyder.

The raccoon knew he was there, for he looked back over his shoulder every few steps. But Jane walked on, content, sucking on a grass stem. No one saw me.

I was sick with fright, and I didn't know why. But I didn't like the sight of that man following my Jane.

"Jane!" I shouted.

Her head jerked up. The raccoon slipped into the brush beside the path. Don Snyder stopped in his tracks.

I ran toward them and grabbed Jane's arm.

"What do you want?" I asked Snyder.

"Hey," he said, holding up both palms in a gesture of mock apology. "No problem. Just making sure the little girl gets back home all right. I found her down by the river. That's not a good place for a retarded kid."

"She's not retarded," I said.

"Yeah?" he responded. "That so? She seems a little strange to me, like her mother."

Aunt Cecile! Where was she?

"There's nothing wrong with anybody," I said.

Adam hurtled up the path behind the man, and I was so relieved to see him that it took a second or two before I realized that he might mean the man harm. Both his hands were clenched into fists.

116

"Adam," I said, and my voice shook. "Is Mother with you?"

Adam gawked at me, and then I saw that he understood. "She's waiting for us inside," he said. He passed Snyder, shouldering him roughly, without apology.

We turned our backs on Snyder and hurried toward the porch. Where was Aunt Cecile?

I burst through the door and found her sitting on the floor in front of a cupboard, smiling, surrounded by old snapshot albums.

"Mama?" she said, astonished. And then her wits returned and she realized who had come in. She got to her feet. "Mary Jack? What's wrong?"

"You let Jane go down to the river alone!" I cried. "What's wrong with you? That awful Snyder was following her. He thinks Jane and you are both retarded, and you act like it! Can't I trust you for even a few minutes?"

Suddenly I was weeping so hard that I thought my heart would burst. Tears gushed from my eyes and my nose ran. Jane disappeared, leaving Adam and Aunt Cecile to stare at me, as if I'd just grown another head.

"I'm tired of taking care of all of you!" I shouted. "You act like babies. I do practically everything, every single day! I hate it that you need somebody to watch over you so that you don't do anything stupid. I'm sick of you!"

I ran toward the bedroom, saw Jane standing in the doorway white-faced, and turned into the bathroom instead, slamming and locking the door behind me.

I don't know how long I sat on the floor, weeping. But it was long enough so that finally Adam pounded on the door and announced that Jane had wet her pants again, not once but twice, and Aunt Cecile needed towels to wipe her off.

Without a word, I unlocked the door and left the bathroom. Jane waited in the hall. Even her shoes were wet.

It was all hopeless, hopeless! I grabbed her hand and hauled her into the bathroom. "You'll need a bath," I said, barely able to speak through the bitterness that choked me.

"I'll give her a bath," Aunt Cecile said.

"She won't let anybody but me do it," I said, resigned.

"Well, she'll have to get used to it," Aunt Cecile said, and she pushed me aside, reaching to turn on the water in the tub.

I expected Jane to run out of the room, but she didn't. Instead, she sat down and pulled off her wet shoes. She avoided my eyes, however.

From the doorway, Adam said, "There's a wet spot on the floor out here."

"So get paper towels and clean it up," Aunt Cecile snapped.

Adam stared, then turned to obey her.

"Mary Jack, go lie down for a while," Aunt Cecile said. "Read a book. I'll call you if I need you."

"That water's too hot for Jane," I said.

Aunt Cecile slipped her hand in the water flowing from the faucet, then said, "It's fine. Do as I say, Mary Jack. Go read a book."

I left the bathroom, but not to read. Instead, I marveled at how good it felt when somebody else was boss.

After Jane's bath, Aunt Cecile called me to the kitchen. "It's time to fix lunch, and I need your help for this," she said.

Her face was deep red. I knew she was embarrassed at my tantrum, and so was I. But I didn't want to apologize. Everything seemed useless anyway. If I was going to end up in another foster home, nothing I did or said would change things now.

"Adam," Aunt Cecile barked, "set the table for lunch. And keep an eye on Jane while you're doing it."

She managed to spread butter on bread by using the knife in her good hand and holding the slice down with the other. Both hands were trembling, but this time I didn't offer to take over.

After Adam left the kitchen with the tableware, Aunt Cecile said, "I'm sorry that your life is so hard, Mary Jack. I didn't realize how dependent we've been and how terrible it is for you. I was wrong to want the summer here without Gerry."

Suddenly the knife slipped from her hand and clattered on the floor. I bent automatically to pick it up.

"Sorry," Aunt Cecile said. "I'm so sorry."

She was sliding over the edge again. For a moment, I'd thought that maybe she had snapped out of her concussion and was well. But here she was, shaking and apologizing, ready to bawl.

She was right. We couldn't spend the whole summer here.

"Fix Aunt Cecile a cup of tea," Adam said from the doorway.

Mary Jack, the maid. I turned to run water in a pan when Aunt Cecile cried out, "I don't need tea! I need to make up my mind about something."

I turned back to look at her. "What are you talking about?"

She shook her head. "I can't believe I let things get this bad. I'd meant to be in charge, but instead you've been stuck with everything, Mary Jack. I thought I'd get well here. Maybe I haven't been trying hard enough."

"It's too late now," I said.

"You're probably right," she said. "We'll tell Matt the truth tomorrow. But I want you to know how sorry I am. If I'd tried harder, things would have been different."

"No, they wouldn't," Adam said. "Every time you

push yourself, you . . ." He stopped, clearly agonized. Shrugging, he looked at me for help.

"He means that you get worse if you try too hard," I said, not caring if I hurt her or not.

But there were some things she could have done, small things like cleaning up the kitchen. And she could have worked at remembering that she'd promised to watch Jane so I could take a walk alone. And she could have practiced things like writing checks and counting money, instead of giving up because Adam and I could work around her shortcomings.

There was no way we could be a family, not even for the summer, no matter how much I tried.

The problem of Don Snyder was a perfect example. I asked Aunt Cecile and Adam what they thought we should do about him.

"He's snooping around," I said. "That's trouble."

"I'll run him off if he comes back," Adam growled.

"You could make things worse," I said as I carried the platter of sandwiches into the main room.

Adam followed with a pitcher of lemonade — without being asked, for once. "How much worse can things get?"

"He knows something is wrong here," Aunt Cecile said. "But I don't see what harm he can do us now, since we're telling Matt everything tomorrow." She put a sandwich on Jane's plate and then helped herself, before pushing the platter toward Adam and me.

121

I didn't want to face the end of everything, but I knew I didn't have a choice. I didn't talk anymore. I'd lost my appetite, but I ate anyway.

And then I remembered the dog. As soon as I told the others about her, they wanted to drop everything and go find her.

"We could take her back to town," I said, hoping that maybe Aunt Cecile and Father Matt could find a home for her.

"Jill hates dogs," Aunt Cecile said. "Maybe Matt could take her to a shelter."

"Oh, no!" I cried. "She needs a real home and a family."

Aunt Cecile looked at me strangely. "There you go again, Mary Jack," she said. "Trying to fix things."

"What's wrong with that?" I demanded.

"Because nothing ever *gets* fixed!" Adam yelled. "Leave the dumb dog out in the woods! She's better off there than she would be in the animal shelter, where they'll kill her."

Jane leaped up and her milk spilled. Her black eyes fixed on Adam, burning into him. Then she ran down the hall.

"Jeez, what did I say?" he complained.

Aunt Cecile covered her eyes with her hand. "This is a . . . a . . . oh, you know what I mean! Blacktime! Nightmare!"

I bit my lip to keep from saying anything, and

went to the kitchen to get the sponge so I could clean up the milk.

Naturally, I thought bitterly, nobody else even thought of it.

In a while, Jane brought out a sketch and pushed it into my hand. She'd drawn the cabin — and looming over it was a scowling man.

"Don't worry," I said automatically. "Don't worry."

After lunch, we took the leftovers to the woods to feed the dog. I led them in single file to the fallen tree. The dog was huddled in her cave, terrified.

I knelt beside the hollow and held out a piece of bread. She sniffed the air and slobber dripped from her mouth. But she wouldn't reach for the bread. I tossed it — and all the other scraps — into the hollow so that she could eat. Watching her gave me a lump in my throat.

"Poor thing," Aunt Cecile murmured. "I wonder how long she's been on her own."

Jane sat beside the hollow and stared without blinking at the dog. After a while, the dog looked straight into Jane's face. The feathery tail flopped gently.

"She likes Jane," Aunt Cecile said.

She understands Jane, I thought. "Come on, let's see if we can get her to come out."

"Leave her!" Adam said. "We'd only scare her. Maybe she'll follow us on her own."

But she didn't. And even though we called her many times, we ended up back at the cabin without her.

But we had company. Don Snyder was back, and this time he had a woman with him.

"This here's my wife," he said, jerking his head toward the stubby, frizzy-haired woman beside him.

She smiled a wide, fake smile that didn't come anywhere near her eyes. "I understand there's a problem here," she said.

She spoke to me.

"What problem?" I asked.

Her eyes flicked toward Aunt Cecile and then Jane. "Should you be on your own here, girlie? I mean, with only your brother for help."

"Someone is coming for us tomorrow," I said.

"You sure?" the woman asked. "Do the people who own this cabin know you've been staying here?"

"We own the cabin," Adam said.

"Yeah, sure," Don Snyder said. "Well, maybe you do and maybe you don't. Down in town, they say that this cabin has been empty for a couple of years. Some people named Percy own it. That's what they say in town."

"My parents," Aunt Cecile said, "were the Percys. I own this now."

"You can prove that?" Mrs. Snyder asked, her eyes bright with meanness.

"You want me to show you the deed?" Aunt Cecile exclaimed. "How dare you! Get out of here right now!"

"We'll be back, to see if you're still here," Mrs. Snyder said, her voice all sweet-sick. "We don't want to cause trouble, but from what Don said, it doesn't seem right that you —"

"Get out of here!" Aunt Cecile cried.

Adam stepped forward and Don Snyder stepped back.

"Violent, too," Mrs. Snyder whispered to her husband, with a significant look aimed at Adam.

I reached out for Adam's arm. "Let's go inside," I said. "They're leaving now."

I felt better after I locked the front door behind us. I watched the Snyders pick their way down the river path, daring them in my mind to look back. I intended to stick out my tongue.

After all, what difference would it make? Tomorrow we would tell Father Matt the truth, and then our adventure in the Monarch River cabin would be over.

In silence, we sat in the main room and looked at each other. Miserable, I gnawed my fingernails.

❧ CHAPTER 11 ❧

By nine o'clock the next morning, the air near the pond seemed almost too heavy and hot to breathe, and the baby ducks were so quiet that a stranger coming by might have thought they were toys, left behind by a child. Mosquitoes hung over the water. They seemed to worry Jane, for she reached for my hand.

The river was the lowest I'd seen it, but the water rushed madly through the rocks. On the bank, the air moved and so it was cooler. Above me, the eagle hung in the bright sky. Jane let go of my hand and shaded her eyes to watch it.

I said goodbye to everything, the eagle, the river, the ducks sheltered under the trees that overhung the pond, the small wild strawberries glistening low to the dark earth, the huckleberry bushes bent down with the burden of their fruit.

Jane tugged the hem of my shirt.

"What?" I asked, and my voice was rough with all the tears I didn't dare shed.

126

She tugged again, and looked to the left of us.

A mother deer and her fawn stood deep in the shadows, watching us. I held my breath for a long moment, afraid to disturb them. When the doe had seen her fill, she nudged the fawn, and the two of them slipped silently into the woods.

Jane looked up — and she almost smiled.

That did it. I burst into tears and knelt beside her. "You don't want to leave, either, do you?" I said to her.

She didn't answer, but then she didn't need to say anything. By now Jane and I could almost read each other's minds.

Or so I thought.

We carried with us a covered dish of cooked hamburger mixed with rice for the stray dog. Aunt Cecile assured me that dogs liked the combination — and after all, we had to get rid of the hamburger some way, since we wouldn't be there for lunch.

The dog was in her den, and I thought that she had almost come to expect us. She wouldn't come out from under the roots to eat until we stepped back, and when she did, she gulped down the food so quickly that I was afraid she'd be sick. When she finished eating, she slid down into the den again and turned to face us.

"Was that good?" I asked.

Her tail flopped once.

"What are we going to do with you?" I said to her.

"You can't stay here, and you won't let anybody grab hold of you. Today's the last day. Couldn't you see your way clear to coming back to the cabin with us?"

She put her head down on her paws, but her eyes were still wary.

"We'll have to drag her out when the time comes," I said to Jane.

Jane looked up into my face, and I had a sudden vision of Adam and me dragging her into the car, too.

Oh, the adventure on Monarch River could have worked! If only I hadn't lost my temper and complained to Aunt Cecile! If only she'd tried to shape up — no, trying made her worse.

If only Don Snyder and his ugly wife hadn't pushed Aunt Cecile into wanting to give up.

No, the main reason the experiment had failed was my selfishness. I'd worked that hard before in other homes. What cast me down so was the way Aunt Cecile would seem all right one moment and completely crazy the next. I never knew what to expect, whether or not I could count on her for anything. I never knew when I'd have two damaged children to care for instead of just one.

The truth was that I'd never dealt very well with surprises of any kind. And Aunt Cecile was a constant surprise.

"Well," I said to Jane, "it'll all be over in another hour. Come on, let's go back to the cabin."

Adam was covering the bedroom furniture with

the dust sheets when we returned. Aunt Cecile, distracted and muttering to herself, was packing her suitcase.

Adam rolled his eyes when he saw me, and cocked his head toward Aunt Cecile. He hadn't looked at her with that disgusted expression since the day he'd heard her use the awful word.

"Give me a hand in the main room, Mary Jack," Adam said.

"I will, in a minute. The dog still won't let me touch her, so I guess we'll have to force her out when it's time to go."

"Leave her," Adam said, his voice tight with anger.

"I can't!" I shouted. "She'll die here."

Aunt Cecile began crying then, the awful, silent kind of crying. I should have done something to comfort her, but I was too full of needs myself to fix any of hers.

I took Jane out to the main room with me, and began pulling the dust sheets out from the cupboard beside the fireplace. Suddenly Jane scuttled down the hall, and almost at the same moment, someone knocked on the open door.

The man was no taller than Adam, with thick gray hair that needed cutting, and a loose, blue T-shirt that hung over his belt. "This the Bradshaw place?" he asked.

My heart hammered under my ribs. "Yes," I said.

He dug a scrap of paper out of his back pocket.

129

"Mrs. Bradshaw here?" he asked. "I got a message for her."

"She's . . ." I hesitated. What should I say? That she wasn't dressed yet? That she was ill?

That she was crazy because she'd hurt her head?

"Yes, what is it?" Aunt Cecile said from behind me.

Her eyes were red, the lids swollen and shiny. But she stood in the middle of the room, straight and calm, and I hoped that she could carry off her act.

The man stepped into the room and held out the note. "Mrs. Bradshaw? This note's for you. Somebody phoned it in to the store, and Jimmy asked me to bring it out here for you so's you wouldn't worry."

Aunt Cecile took the note and said, "Thank you for your trouble. It's a long walk from the road. Mary Jack, get my purse."

"No, ma'am," the man said, backing toward the door. "I don't need a tip. Just being neighborly, that's all. I remember Mrs. Percy, your mother. I cut wood for her when I was a boy. She was always good to me."

Aunt Cecile smiled her crooked smile, and her eyes filled with tears.

Oh, no, I thought. But it was all right, because the man said, "I was sure sorry to hear that she'd passed on, Mrs. Bradshaw."

And then he left. I was dizzy with relief.

"What does the note say?" I asked.

Aunt Cecile unfolded it awkwardly with her good hand, and stared at it.

"I can't read it," she said.

I was going to reach for it, and then I pulled back my hand. "Try," I said. Sudden meanness sprang up in me, made even worse by the heat, I suppose.

She covered her bad eye with her bad hand and studied the note. Finally she said, "It's a message from Matt. He can't come. Someone in the parish died early this morning."

Excitement filled me, and guilt drove it out. "I'm sorry somebody's dead," I said, "but we can stay a little longer now. Does the note say when he'll be coming?"

Aunt Cecile's mouth twisted. "Next Saturday."

I was so stunned that I didn't even know how to react. Even Adam was silent.

Jane crept up behind me and took my hand, reminding me of the responsibilities here that someone had to take on.

"I guess we're not going home today after all," I told her.

"Ha," Adam said. "If Snyder comes back, we may have to leave by ourselves."

Aunt Cecile was wringing her hands again, a bad sign. But then, to my surprise, she said, "We can manage. *I* can manage. If I make up my mind, and don't push too hard, and don't let myself get upset when I forget things or can't find the right word, then we'll be fine. At least until next Saturday."

"But that awful man has fun scaring us," I said. "He'll be back. People like him always come back. And then . . . and then . . ."

"Maybe he won't," Adam said. "The campground people are having this big Fourth of July celebration. He'll forget about us."

I had forgotten the Fourth of July. "Maybe," I said, but I wasn't convinced. Don Snyder was the bogeyman to me.

We stripped the dust covers off the beds, made ourselves a picnic, and ate beside the river. Across from us, on the other shore, an old man cast out his fishing line over and over into a pool below the rapids, and he didn't seem to care that he didn't catch anything. We watched him, not talking, letting the voice of the water erase our frights.

When Jane's eyelids drooped, we took her back to the cabin for a nap. Adam intended sneaking away again — I could tell by the way he sidled toward the door — but Aunt Cecile stopped him.

"Adam, I have a job for you," she said.

"I've already cut kindling for tonight," he said. "But it's so hot, I don't think we'll need it."

"I'm not talking about kindling," Aunt Cecile said. "I want you to help me learn numbers again."

Adam stared. So did I.

"What do you mean, learn numbers?" I asked.

She grimaced. "The awful truth is, I don't think I can manage my checkbook without help. I looked at it this morning, and it doesn't make a lot of sense to me. I'm not talking about the checks — I think I've figured out what to write and where to write it. It's the numbers that confuse me."

She looked at us with an expression that I would have expected to see on the face of the dog hiding under the dead tree.

"Actually," she said, "sometimes numbers don't make a damn bit of sense, and I can't see the point of the whole messy business."

"You mean you forgot how to count?" I asked, horrified.

She rubbed her forehead, as if this would help. "That's not it exactly," she said. "I can count." And she did, rapidly to twelve, but then she skipped to fifteen, and Adam began laughing.

"Be quiet," she said to him. "It's not funny. I know what I did was wrong, but if I get nervous, I can't straighten it out."

"I knew a girl who had problems like that, in sixth grade," I said. "I tried to help her, but we could only go so far and then she'd get upset and forget everything. The teacher put her in a class for kids who were called learning disabled."

Aunt Cecile flushed a little. "Well, that describes me, I guess. The doctors said I'd have trouble, but they said I could learn again, that the damage wasn't permanent. Now we'll have to see if it is or isn't."

"But how?" Adam asked.

"You'll give me lessons, just as if I were a child again," Aunt Cecile said.

"But I don't know anything about teaching!" Adam protested. "Get Mary Jack to do it."

"I'm getting you to do it!" Aunt Cecile cried. "Mary Jack has been stuck with everything. Now you and I will make up for it."

"Jeez," Adam whined.

"Jeez indeed," Aunt Cecile said cheerfully. "Let's get busy. You show me what you know about simple math."

"That won't take long," I muttered, on my way to the kitchen for a glass of water.

Who would believe this? Everybody in the cabin was crazy, including me. If you boxed us all up together, I thought, we wouldn't make a good half-wit.

During the math lesson, I sneaked away and visited the dog. I tossed bits of cheese to her, and once she almost accepted a piece from my fingers.

"We're not going away," I said to her. "Not yet, anyway."

Flap, flap, went her tail, and she rolled her eyes.

"You belong down at the cabin with us," I said. "You'd be the smartest one there."

As if she understood, she shifted her position so that her back was toward me, and she sighed. No way, she seemed to say. Go home, Mary Jack. I'm better off living under a dead tree.

CHAPTER 12

The Fourth of July is always a noisy holiday in Seattle, but I hadn't expected much racket in Monarch River. I was wrong. The campground people and their visitors raised enough uproar to drive the crows out of the woods. Besides that, the little town itself seemed to attract people from all over, and most of them wanted to spend part of the day walking along the river.

They started coming before noon. The first ones sent Adam running for the cabin to warn Aunt Cecile of trespassers.

"It's all right," she told us. "Most of them don't do much more than stare at the cabin as they walk by. A few will come closer, but we always sent them on their way with a smile and a caution about the bears in the woods."

"What bears?" I demanded, goose bumps rising on my arms.

Aunt Cecile laughed. "There haven't been bears around here for fifty years, but the city people don't

136

know that, so they usually go straight back to town.''

Adam let out a sigh. "You scared me for a minute," he said. "I was thinking about Goldie, down there under the hollow tree."

I gawked at him. "You named the dog? You're calling her Goldie? I thought you didn't care what happened to her."

"I don't," he growled. "But even a stray dog needs a name."

"Sure," I said, grinning at him.

"He's right," Aunt Cecile said. "She'll be Goldie, and we hope that before much longer she won't be a stray. Maybe by Saturday we can get her to trust us."

Saturday. The word cast a shadow over the day. Father Matt would be coming on Saturday. And even before that, Don Snyder might come back.

Jane didn't like the fireworks much, and retreated to the bedroom with her tablet and crayons. When she came out again, she presented me with a horrifying picture.

She'd drawn Goldie in her hole, with bright red stars in the air all around.

"The dog," I said, holding the picture up for the others to see. "Jane remembered that she'll be afraid of fireworks."

We rushed from the cabin, and for the first time Aunt Cecile locked the door behind us. "Just in case," she said.

When we reached the dog's hiding place, we

thought at first that she wasn't there, for we couldn't see her under the tangle of roots. But Jane crawled down into the hole and suddenly stood up, wide-eyed.

"She's way in the back?" I asked.

Jane got out to make room for me. I let myself down into the hollow and crouched. Yes, there was the dog. But something was wrong. She was not only terrified, she was in pain. When she saw me, she let out a great groan that ended in a pitiful whine.

I climbed out of the hollow. "I think she's been hurt."

"Let me look," Adam said, and he shoved me out of the way.

He was bigger than I was, and he had trouble wedging himself far enough into the hollow to see what was wrong. When he came out, he was pale.

"She's having her puppies. One of them is already born, but I think it's dead. Something's not right. She oughtn't to be crying so much."

"Oh, lord," Aunt Cecile said. "Can you get her out?"

"I might hurt her if I touch her," Adam said.

"She's already in pain," Aunt Cecile said. "I don't think you can make it worse. But we've got to help her — we can't leave her there to suffer and maybe die."

Adam shoved himself deep into the hollow again, lying on his stomach, murmuring soothing words to the dog. After long moments, he reached something back to me, something small and tan.

I took the dead puppy in both hands and burst into tears.

"Here, quick," Aunt Cecile said. "Maybe I can do something."

But when she took the poor little thing from me, she shook her head slowly. "No, it's cold already. How awful."

Adam was inching his way backward, saying, "It's okay, it's okay."

"Have you got her?" I asked.

He didn't answer me, but kept up his steady reassurance to the dog. At last he pulled her free, and we saw her terrified eyes.

"We have to get her to a vet," Adam said.

"There isn't one in Monarch River," I said. "We know what's on every street, and there isn't a vet here."

"The nearest would be twenty miles away, maybe more," Aunt Cecile said. "And today's a holiday. The office would be closed. No, we'll take her to Al's farm. He'll know what to do. He's wonderful with animals."

She gave Adam, who could run fastest, the front-door key, and he bolted back to the cabin for the car keys. The rest of us petted and crooned to the suffering dog. Occasionally her golden sides would heave with a terrible effort, but no puppies were born.

I knew Adam would run as fast as he could, but he seemed to take forever before he returned with the car keys. Quickly, he scooped up the dog and we followed him to the car.

We were hemmed in by another car that had parked too close behind us. "We'll never get out!" I cried.

"Oh, yes, we will!" Aunt Cecile shouted. "Drive over the brooms — the brushes — the *bushes*!"

Jane and I crawled in back, and Adam settled the dog on the second seat. Then he and Aunt Cecile jumped in front, Adam started the car, and he did exactly what Aunt Cecile had told him to do. He drove it out into the bushes, crushing them under the wheels, and circled around the car that blocked our path.

"Jackass," Aunt Cecile said, with a fierce scowl for the other car.

Adam shot her an admiring look, and we tore down the long road to the first intersection, where Adam turned east. He remembered the way to the farm.

It took a forever and another forever after that, even though Aunt Cecile said the farm was only six miles away. At last we pulled through an open gate, bumped down a dirt driveway, and stopped in front of a ranch house with a long porch.

Adam and Aunt Cecile piled out of the car and ran

toward the porch. But Al came from around behind the house and stopped them.

"What's wrong?" I heard him shout. "What's happened?"

Aunt Cecile explained quickly, and Al trotted toward the car. He bent inside, examined the dog, and clicked his tongue.

"The puppies are stuck," he said. "She needs a vet."

"But where will we find one today?" Aunt Cecile cried.

Al gathered the dog up in his arms, in spite of her struggles, and carried her away toward the big barn behind his house. Another man came out of the barn, and Al stopped to talk to him.

Adam and Aunt Cecile had followed Al, but Jane didn't want to go, and dug in stubbornly when I tried to force her along the path.

"Don't make me carry you," I said. "I want to see what's going on."

But Jane fell to the ground and grabbed me by the ankles, keeping me from taking a step.

"Jane, you make me so mad sometimes!" I shouted. "Stop that and get up."

She hung on tighter. I saw Adam and Aunt Cecile disappear into the barn behind the men.

"I want to see what happens to the dog," I said. "Let go of me or I'll never read to you from the animal book again."

Jane let go. I hauled her to her feet and dragged her to the barn.

Aunt Cecile came out, pale and tense. "Don't go in, Mary Jack," she said. "The other man, that Tony, said he knows what to do. He said he can help the dog without operating on her."

"Is he a vet?" I asked.

She shook her head. "No, but he says he's helped animals before when this happens."

Inside the barn, the dog cried out terribly, and Aunt Cecile gasped.

"He's hurting her!" I wept.

"He has to, to save her," Aunt Cecile said. "But I couldn't watch. I couldn't."

"Is Adam watching?" I asked.

She nodded. "Al wanted him to stay, to help with the puppies if any are still alive."

The dog cried out again. I couldn't stand to listen to her, and Jane was clutching me around the waist so hard that she was hurting me.

"I'm taking Jane back to the porch," I said.

Aunt Cecile nodded absently. She was listening to the men's voices in the barn.

Jane nearly pulled me back to the porch, and when we got there, she sat down on a step and covered her ears with her hands. I considered doing the same thing, but I couldn't hear the dog anymore, and so I just sat there, looking out over the field where the mares and colts had taken shelter from the sun under wide-spreading maples and birches.

As time passed and the trees' shadows moved, the horses moved, too, lazily. Occasionally I heard bird-calls from the woods. And sometimes, far away, I heard fireworks.

After a long while, Adam and Aunt Cecile came around the side of the house.

"Is she all right?" I asked quickly.

Aunt Cecile nodded. "But only one of the puppies was alive. The other four were dead."

I put my head down on my knees and wept. Poor stray dog. Poor Goldie. Poor dead babies.

"Al's going to keep her here," Aunt Cecile said. "He'll have the vet come out to check her over, and she'll stay in the barn until she gets used to him. Now she has a home and everything will be all right for her."

Except that most of her babies were dead. And she'd be living with Al instead of with me.

Oh, well, I thought. What could I have done for her? I couldn't have kept her anyway. Even if I got to stay with the Percys, they wouldn't put up with a dog. Aunt Cecile would be going back to her apartment someday, and she couldn't keep a dog there. And Adam, well, who knew what would happen to him? It was better for the dog — for Goldie — to stay on this beautiful farm, with Al and his horses.

Al joined us then, smiling. "That's a fine dog," he said. "She'll be okay, I think, and so will her little girl. I trust Tony about these things. Goldie's her name? Is that right?"

We nodded solemnly.

"The pup's not yellow like her. She's more of a gray color, so Tony, he says why don't we call her Silver? What do you think?"

Adam smiled and nodded. Aunt Cecile said, "Wonderful. Thank you, Al."

But Jane and I huddled together, and I knew she was thinking what I was thinking. Who would name the other puppies, the ones who died without anybody ever wanting them except their mother?

"We'll name them, you and I," I whispered in her ear. "And you draw pictures of them. Can you do that?"

She nodded. She had never nodded before.

I hugged her. "Thank you, Jane," I said.

Aunt Cecile had brought the dead puppy in the car, and so now Al and Adam buried it and the others in a corner of the field, near a place where pale pink wild roses grew.

"We'll call the first one Rose," I whispered to Jane. She nodded again.

We drove home slowly, silently. The fireworks were worse, and there were more people on the roads. By the time we reached our own road, I was beginning to wonder how long this day would stretch out, for it seemed to me that we'd endured a whole hot, noisy summer in this one afternoon.

At the end of our road, Don Snyder was getting into his car. As soon as he saw us, he got back out again.

He hooked his thumbs inside his belt and stared knowingly at Adam. "A little young to be driving a car, aren't you, kid?"

"I'm old enough —" began Adam.

At the same moment, Aunt Cecile said, "He's driving under my supervision."

"Well, which is it, folks?" Don Snyder asked. "Old enough or not old enough? I can see by the brush at the side of the road how he took out of here. Didn't care what he ran over. Guess we're all lucky he didn't slam that old wreck into one of our cars." He lifted one corner of his lip in a mean smile. "Unless you were driving, Mrs. Bradshaw. But then, I guess you don't drive. My wife says you look to her like you had some sort of stroke. That true?"

He scratched his head then, as if he was thinking things over. "'Course, you told us last Friday that you were leaving here the next day. Guess that wasn't the truth. But I can't think why anybody would lie that way to a neighbor. Not unless they had something to hide. Like maybe they didn't have a right to that cabin after all. Like maybe they broke in or something."

"Come along, children," Aunt Cecile said, standing straight, with a haughty set to her shoulders. "We have a lot to do back at the cabin. Adam, you have the front-door key?" She leveled a cold look at Snyder. "We have to lock our doors these days," she said. "It's not the way it used to be, when a woman could trust her neighbors not to steal from her."

And with that, Aunt Cecile snatched up Jane's hand and started down the path toward the cabin.

Adam made much of locking up the car, but he didn't look at Snyder. I did, though.

He was grinning. He liked making people nervous, scaring them a little, leaving them to wonder what he might do or say next.

I trudged after the others, and when I looked back, I saw that Snyder was still watching, still smiling his evil, rat-faced smile.

◆ CHAPTER 13 ◆

I should have suspected that Adam would react to our ugly neighbor in one way or another. But I was so tired, and so glad to be home, that I ignored his brooding silence and went ahead washing off Jane's hands and face while Aunt Cecile busied herself in the kitchen. I could tell she was upset, because she was dropping more things than usual.

No one was hungry, but we picked at sandwiches and finished a jug of lemonade while we sat on the porch steps, listening to the river. And the fireworks.

"It gets worse as the day goes along," Aunt Cecile said.

Jane scooted next to me, leaning close. I slid my arm over her shoulders. "Will it go on all night?" I asked Aunt Cecile.

"No. The city people start home long before midnight, thank goodness." Aunt Cecile's sigh was heavy, drawn out.

Adam, elbows on knees, stared off into the forest as

if he expected to see something there. "What happens to the animals?" he asked. "Don't they get scared?"

"I'm sure they do," Aunt Cecile said. "They probably think humans are insane."

This time Adam sighed. "They are," he said.

Later, when twilight was nearly ready to slip into night, we ate again, inside. Cold fried chicken and potato salad and sliced tomatoes. Afterward, Adam turned on the TV, restlessly switching channels. When he finally settled on an old movie, Jane crept up in a chair and watched with him. Neither of them acknowledged the presence of the other.

Aunt Cecile, watching them from the kitchen doorway, said, "I wonder what their lives have been like."

She had spoken so softly that I'd barely heard her. I straightened up from rinsing plates and said, "Adam doesn't say much about himself, and Jane doesn't ever talk."

"Did my brother ever tell you about them?"

I shook my head. "I don't believe Father Matt knows anything about Jane — nobody does. But Adam lived in another part of Seattle, and one of his neighbors — or maybe it was a teacher — anyway, somebody got in touch with this church group that finds foster homes for kids. I think his mother drank, and he doesn't have a father."

Aunt Cecile nodded. "And what about you, Mary Jack?"

There had been a time when I would have launched into my story of the different foster homes I had lived in and how much I wanted my own family. But I'd had time to think. My story was nothing more than a list of people who hadn't wanted me for one reason or another. I wouldn't have a family, not ever. And so there was no reason to make myself look bad again.

"I didn't know my parents," I said, while I ran water in the sink. "I've always lived in foster homes. Why don't you go in the other room and watch TV?"

"No, I'd rather talk to you," Aunt Cecile said. She hooked a stool out from under the breakfast bar with her foot and perched on it. "Matt cares about you very much, you know," she said. "He told me that without you, he couldn't have kept Jane. She would have been put in an institution for mentally handicapped children."

I turned to stare at her. "Jane's not retarded."

"I know. But the bad things that happened to her have affected her mind. You made it possible for her to stay with my brother and his wife."

Apparently she hadn't figured out yet that when Father Matt faced up to the problems here, we'd be hauled back to the Percys only to be split up and sent to separate foster homes. Didn't she realize that Jill had made things clear to Father Matt before we left Seattle? Either he got rid of us for the summer or she'd get rid of us permanently.

"I always wanted children of my own," Aunt Cecile went on.

I was embarrassed by this. And I didn't want to hear more painful things about her. But I had no idea how to stop her. Outside, in the distance, thunder rolled.

"But David and I never had children," she said. "I guess it's a blessing, because now they'd be without a father, and who knows what would have happened to them these past months since . . ."

I glanced at her from the corner of my eye, dreading what I'd see. Her face was lopsided. Tears dripped from her chin. She was sliding downhill into one of her black moods again.

"I'll fix tea," I said quickly, my voice too loud.

Adam appeared in the doorway, silent and watchful.

"She's all right," I told him as I ran water into the teakettle. "It's been a hard day."

"Yeah," he said. He looked long and hard at Aunt Cecile, but I couldn't read his expression.

"Go back and watch TV with Jane," I said.

"Yeah." He padded away without a backward glance.

I made a whole pot of tea for Aunt Cecile and settled her down at the table in the main room, facing

150

the open door and the dark woods beyond. "Listen. No fireworks. We can hear the river again."

The teacup wobbled in her hand, but she listened and smiled her crooked smile.

Darn that Don Snyder.

I slept hard that night, and woke later than usual to the sound of rain on the roof. Aunt Cecile and Jane were already in the kitchen. Aunt Cecile mixed eggs and milk awkwardly with her good hand, and Jane crouched on the floor, drawing.

"You should have called me," I complained.

"You were worn out," Aunt Cecile said. "I'm fixing scrambled eggs and toast. Is that okay with you?"

"Sure, but Adam's not crazy about eggs," I said.

"Go knock on his door and ask him what he wants," she said. "And ask him to build a fire. That rain makes the cabin cold."

On my way I passed Jane, who glanced up at me with a frightened expression.

"Hey," I said. "What's the problem?"

She bent over her drawing again, so I went on down the hall to ask Adam what he wanted to eat and get him started on a fire.

He didn't answer when I knocked, so I opened his door and found the room empty.

Empty.

The bunk he'd been using hadn't been slept in that night, but the car keys lay on the pillow.

I yanked open the closet door and found that his few clothes were gone.

I'd been expecting this, but now I felt exactly the way I did when someone once kicked a soccer ball into my stomach.

For a moment, I couldn't think of what to do. When Aunt Cecile found out, she'd go off into orbit again, and that would leave me alone with two people who couldn't help themselves at all. But I couldn't get away with lying to her about him. If I said that he wasn't hungry, she'd want to know if he was sick. If I said he'd gone out into the woods already, she'd be suspicious.

My heart was beating so hard that I couldn't hear myself think. Darn Adam! Why did he pick now to do this? Selfish brat.

I had no choice, so I grabbed the keys, marched to the kitchen, and said, "Adam's run off. I knew he would, sooner or later. But it won't make any difference to us now, so let's eat. Then I'll start a fire." I dropped the keys on the counter.

At first I thought Aunt Cecile hadn't heard me. Her back was to me. She stood very still for a long time, and then she turned and I saw that her eyes were glazed with fright and tears.

"Don't you dare get sick on me!" I cried. "You can't! You have to stay *all right,* because I can't do everything alone!"

Jane flung her arms around my legs, holding on tight.

Aunt Cecile blinked hard. She opened her mouth to speak, then changed her mind and turned back to the stove.

"Please set the table," she said, her voice strained.

I let out the breath I'd been holding, and tried to get loose from Jane's grip, but I couldn't.

"Let go, Jane," I said. "Our eggs will get cold if I don't set the table right away." My voice was trembling, which angered me, because I certainly didn't want to get caught bawling now.

I had to bend down and pry Jane off. She was clutching her picture, and suddenly she thrust it at me.

I smoothed it out and saw that she'd drawn Adam, going out the door with a bag in one hand.

She'd known that he ran away.

"Oh, Jane," I said, and I bent to kiss her. "It's going to be all right. I promise."

Her black eyes held me.

"I *promise*," I repeated.

She blinked and let me go.

I didn't dare think about what might happen next. And that was just as well, because the day didn't improve.

We'd scarcely finished breakfast when Don Snyder pounded on our door, in such a fury that I was afraid he'd break one of the glass panes before I could open it.

"Where's that boy?" he shouted at us.

Now what? What could Adam have done, I wondered, to send the awful man here in a rage? I turned to see how Aunt Cecile was taking this.

She rose to her feet and folded her napkin. "What seems to be your problem, Mr. Snyder?"

He advanced on her, his wet hair plastered to his forehead, his jacket streaming water. "He busted out my car windows, that's what he did," he shouted. "Windshield, everything!"

"And he signed his name to his vandalism when he was done?" Aunt Cecile asked.

That stopped Snyder. "What? What are you talking about?"

"How do you know Adam was the one?" Aunt Cecile asked.

"It had to be him!" Snyder shouted.

"Prove it," she said.

"Get him out here and I will!" Snyder cried. "Where is he? You, Adam, get out here!"

"Adam, stay where you are!" Aunt Cecile called out, her voice sharp.

Then she stepped forward, her finger pointing at Snyder until she almost touched the front of his jacket. "Get out of this house or I will report you to the police," she said. "How dare you harass me in my own home, in front of these girls? Get out, now."

154

And then she pressed her finger against his jacket and he backed up. His wet face was livid.

"It was him," he said. "I know it."

"Out," Aunt Cecile said. She slammed the door the moment he backed out to the porch.

And then her face collapsed crookedly and her mouth shook.

I leaped forward and grabbed her arm. Behind her, through the windows, I could see that Snyder had darted out into the rain.

"He's gone. You did good." I helped her to a chair, and when I was sure that she wouldn't cry, I went off to find Jane. She had disappeared the moment Snyder walked in the door.

She had wedged herself between the bathroom basin cabinet and the tub, facing the wall. When I reached out to touch her, she flinched.

"He's gone," I said. "You can come out. Don't you know that I wouldn't let him hurt you? I'd kill him before I'd let him do anything to you."

She made a mewing sound, a sick-cat sound, but I was glad because it was the first I'd ever heard from her.

I knelt on the floor behind her. "Jane, I love you so much. I know you can talk. Can't you trust me enough to tell me your real name? Or if you want to keep it a secret, couldn't you tell me that you like me? I'd be so glad. I really need a little sister right now."

Jane backed out and turned to face me, but only

her eyes spoke. She loved me and she was my sister. Until we were separated, anyway.

I led her back to the main room, put her on one sofa with a blanket spread over her and Aunt Cecile on the other, cozied up under a plaid afghan. The cabin was so chilly that I needed a jacket. Or a fire.

And naturally the kindling box was empty.

"I'm going out to get kindling," I told Aunt Cecile.

She rose up halfway, shaking her head. "Don't use the . . . the . . ."

"Axe," I finished crisply. "No, of course not. I'll take some of the kindling Adam left in the shed."

I banged out of the door fast, before she went off into one of her waking nightmares again. They'd just have to manage! And so would I, because I already knew for a fact that Adam never left kindling in the shed.

The shed door was slightly ajar, and I stepped inside out of the rain. The axe leaned against the wall. I could take it out in the rain, prop a piece of firewood on the old stump, and chop kindling the way I'd watched Adam do. Or I could rig up something in the shed, out of the rain, and stay dry.

I chose staying dry.

I set a piece of firewood on end on the bare ground inside the shed, watched it fall over, swore, and set it up again. Then I raised the axe high, swung it down in an arc, and sank it into my leg just above my ankle.

❧ CHAPTER 14 ❧

At first I felt only the thud of the blow, not the sharp pain. I gasped, and in the same split second, I was glad that I'd hit myself with the blunt side of the axe.

But then I looked down and saw that I was wrong. I let go of the axe and the weight of the handle pulled it out of my leg. Blood gushed, instantly drenching my sock and shoe.

And the pain hit. I couldn't draw my breath. Stunned, I bent double. My blood was pouring out on the ground.

I screamed then, screamed and screamed. When I tried to hop out of the shed on my good leg, the pain increased. I clung to the door, half out in the rain, and screamed for Aunt Cecile. Only, in my agony I cried, *"Mama!"*

She heard me, Aunt Cecile. Somehow, in spite of her dizzy mind and the rain hitting the roof, she heard me and came running, with Jane scuttling behind, dragging her blanket through the mud.

"Oh my God!" Aunt Cecile cried when she saw what I had done.

I thought that I would die there. I wasn't sure I could count on Aunt Cecile for anything, but she yanked off her belt, wrapped it around my leg above the knee, and pulled it tight.

"Now," she said, bending down to study my horrid wound. "I need you to lie down so I can get a better look — yes, like that."

She helped me lower myself to the ground, and then she knelt to look closely at the damage I had done myself.

"Jane," she said, "we have to take Mary Jack to the hospital. Go back to the cabin and get my purse and the car keys. My purse is in the bedroom and the keys are on the kitchen counter."

"No!" I cried. "If you take me to the hospital, they'll call Father Matt and everything will be over with today! He'll separate you and Jane and me. It will all be over with."

"No, it won't," she said. "I'll handle it. Let me show you."

She sent Jane off and spread Jane's dirty blanket over me, which kept off some of the rain.

"My leg hurts," I said.

"I'm sure it does," Aunt Cecile said. "Cry if you want to. I would." She brushed my hair out of my eyes. "When Jane gets here, you'll have to work hard getting out to the car, okay? I don't think I can carry you."

I nodded. We'd never make it, I thought. We'd end up begging for help from the summer people — or even Snyder — and the more people who knew about our trouble, the worse off we'd be.

Jane flew back, purse in one hand, car keys in the other.

Aunt Cecile helped me to my feet, threw the blanket around my shoulders, and then, supporting me on one side, helped me walk. Jane ran ahead with the purse and car keys, and was out of sight in moments.

"You can do this, I know you can," Aunt Cecile said.

"Yes," I said. I looked up into the rain for a moment, letting the drops cool my burning eyes, and then concentrated on the path in front of us.

"I should have had a phone put in," Aunt Cecile said.

"I'll be fine," I gasped. In my mind, I ran ahead of the pain, free of our awkward, slow progress. Yes, I could see Jane in my mind, with the car doors open, holding out Aunt Cecile's purse. And now we were in the car and now we were somewhere — where? — in a hospital and somebody was doing something about the awful cut on my leg.

We passed the cabin — door standing open — and the pond. Now we hopped and struggled and grunted along the overgrown path. One quarter of a mile.

And yes, there was Jane, with the car doors open — all four of them — holding out Aunt Cecile's purse.

And then I was in the back seat, wrapped in a different blanket now, a dry one, and the car was humming along roads, humming on a highway.

Aunt Cecile was driving — Aunt Cecile, who had double vision and one bad arm, who couldn't count change or remember words.

I saw red pulsing and throbbing inside my eyelids. "Aunt Cecile?" I asked, fearful of how she would answer me.

"How are you getting along, Mary Jack?" she asked in return.

"Fine."

"We're almost at the Carson Valley Hospital," she said. "Another couple of blocks."

I opened my eyes and saw through the rain-slashed windows that we were moving through a town. Everything would be all right.

Two hours later, after I'd been x-rayed, stitched, bandaged, injected, and lectured about axes, the doctor who took care of me asked me if I had any questions.

"Don't I need a blood transfusion?" I asked.

He cocked his head. "Do you think you need one?"

160

"I bled all over the place," I said.

"I bet you did," he said. "No, you have plenty left. Lucky for you that you didn't cut an artery, though. The bad news is that you'll have a scar that people will be asking questions about for the rest of your life. Then you can tell them not to be stupid with axes. You'll have a mission. See, Miss Mary Jack Bradshaw? Everything turns out all right in the end."

He'd struck me dumb, but he didn't seem to notice. He walked away then, as if he hadn't just said something that electrified me. He'd called me Mary Jack *Bradshaw*.

The nurse helped me sit up. Aunt Cecile, her clothes still damp, got up from the chair where she'd been sitting with Jane on her lap.

"It's all right for me to take her home?" she asked the nurse.

"The doctor said so," the nurse responded, sounding busy and impatient. "But you'll have to bring her back to have the stitches out. And she needs to take the antibiotics. If you have any problems, give us a call." She gave Aunt Cecile a disgusted look. "And for heaven's sake, cut your own kindling after this." Then she left us alone together in the curtained cubicle.

My leg throbbed steadily. The bandage was the only clean part of me. But my mind was set on one thing.

"You told them my name was Bradshaw?" I asked Aunt Cecile.

"I thought it would make everything easier," she said. "I said you were my daughter."

Jane touched my shoulder, as if she was asking a question.

"It doesn't hurt as much now," I said.

Before we left the hospital, I was given crutches, a bottle of pills, and still another lecture about playing with axes. Outside, the rain had stopped. In the west, the sky glistened, pearl pink and pale blue.

"Let's go home," Aunt Cecile said. "I'm starved."

But we didn't go straight back to the cabin. On the way, Aunt Cecile slowed the car and said, "I'm having trouble, Mary Jack. I think I'm all used up."

I thought I knew what she meant. "Stop by the side of the road," I said. I was remembering the accident she'd been in. We didn't need another.

"We're close to Al's," she said. "I'm going there."

I raised up. "Don't tell him anything!" I cried.

The car wobbled along the road and Aunt Cecile didn't answer.

Not now, I thought. Not now, when we're so close to making it. If nothing worse happened, and we could convince Father Matt that she was well again — or almost well — and we didn't need Gerry or Adam or anybody, then maybe we could spend the rest of the summer here, and Jane and I wouldn't lose each other.

I imagined how I'd tell Father Matt how Aunt Cecile handled my accident, how she drove us to the hospital and home again, just as if she was normal. But she had to keep a grip on herself.

"Please don't tell," I said again.

When we stopped in front of the farmhouse, Al came out to greet us. "The dog's fine," he said, leaning in the car to talk to me. "She and the pup are snuggled up in the barn, happy as can be. Want to get out and see her?"

"Al, she can't," Aunt Cecile said. "I'm bringing her home from the hospital. She cut her leg this morning, and she can't do much walking right now."

"Well, what can I do to help?" Al said instantly.

Aunt Cecile hesitated a moment, then said, "I'm afraid getting her back to the cabin is a bit more than I can handle right now, and I wondered if you could follow me back there and carry the child in from the road."

"You bet," he said, and he ran toward the truck parked around the side of the house.

"Can you drive back to the cabin?" I asked in a low voice.

"I think so, if someone's following, so I'm sure I'll get help if I need it." Aunt Cecile turned the car down the driveway. "And I knew we'd need help getting you through the woods."

My leg ached and my head seemed to be on fire. All the way to the cabin, I willed Aunt Cecile to stay calm, no matter how bad things got for her. Don't cry, I thought. Don't shake. Don't try talking because if you mix up words, you'll freak out again. Don't panic.

We arrived. Aunt Cecile parked sloppily, partway in the brush, but I didn't care if Snyder got mad when he saw. I had the satisfaction of looking out my window and seeing what had happened to all of his windows. He was right. Every one was broken.

Good for you, Adam. But I wish you hadn't run off.

Al carried me easily, as if I didn't weigh an ounce. Aunt Cecile followed, with my crutches. And Jane trailed behind, still holding Aunt Cecile's purse in her fists.

It didn't take Al any time at all to settle us in. He put me on a sofa, and while Aunt Cecile helped me change into my nightgown, he built a hot fire to warm up the cabin.

Jane simply stared at him. She didn't take her eyes off him, although she kept out of his way. He, in turn, elaborately ignored her. I wondered at this.

But then I saw his plan. She felt safer with him if he didn't look directly at her. It gave her a head start.

"Let me fix you folks something to eat," Al said finally. "You missed lunch, and by now you must be hungry."

"No, thank you," Aunt Cecile said, too quickly. She sounded as if she was trying to hurry him out. That wasn't a good idea.

"I insist," he said. "Won't take me a minute or two to whip up something. Soup and sandwiches, or maybe chili and toast?" He looked at me and crinkled his eyes. "Hey, woodsman, you name it."

"Chili and toast," I said. That would be quickest. And maybe, with luck, Aunt Cecile would decide that she needed to change both her clothes and Jane's — and stay out of this part of the house for as long as possible.

But she stood, uncertain and bewildered, at the end of the sofa, looking down at me.

"Jane's awfully dirty and her clothes are probably still damp," I said. "And nobody's taken her to the bathroom for a million years."

"Yes," Aunt Cecile said. "Yes." And she reached for Jane and led her down the hall.

I could smell canned chili warming on the stove. My mouth watered.

"Now that we're alone, young lady," Al said softly.

He was standing directly behind me.

My heart sank. "Yes?" I said.

"Suppose you tell me what the hell is going on around here?"

"I don't know what you're talking about," I said.

He changed position and knelt beside me. "Don't

bull me, little lady. You know exactly what I'm talking about. I knew the first time I saw you that you were the one who had it all together. Something's wrong with Cecile. What is it?"

I squeezed my eyes shut, hoping he'd disappear. He didn't.

I told him everything. I was too tired to go on with the struggle. One way or another, I would lose my home again, and I decided that I might as well get it over with.

When I finished — and I admit that I was bawling at the end of my story — Al squeezed my shoulder once and said, "You did a fine job. Don't give up yet. You need to get some food into you, and a little sleep. And maybe a little help won't hurt right about now."

Aunt Cecile and Jane came out then, in clean clothes. But Aunt Cecile was shaky and close to tears. Jane clutched her tablet to her chest and gave Al a smoldering look as she passed him to take her place at the table.

I had my meal on a tray, smoking hot chili and wheat toast with just the right amount of butter on it. I eavesdropped on the table talk, hoping that nothing would go wrong, that Al wouldn't tell Aunt Cecile that I'd blabbed. She'd go to pieces.

But instead, he droned on and on about his farm, the horses and their babies, his apple crop, the creek that overflowed into his driveway every winter. Aunt Cecile never said much of anything but "Oh, really," and "How nice." His voice, low and rumbling, almost like a stray cat's purr, soothed me into a doze.

I awoke with a start, to hear the clock striking nine.

"I was asleep!" I cried, sitting up, only to be wrenched back by pain from the injury I'd forgotten.

Aunt Cecile, deep in an armchair, said, "You've been sleeping for a long time. How do you feel? Are you hungry again?"

"We just ate," I said.

"You ate hours ago," she said. "Since then Jane and I had leftover chicken made into a salad and nearly all the rest of the bread. I'll fix you a sandwich if you want one."

"No, thanks. Where's Al?"

"He's been gone for hours," she said. "What a nice man. He did the dishes after dinner. I don't think he noticed anything wrong, though. But of course, how could he? I didn't remember him being such a talkative person."

I grinned secretly, then said, "Jane in bed?"

"Yes, without a bath. I didn't trust myself to manage her and hot water both. She didn't mind. She drew you a picture."

She got up and took a sheet of paper off the mantel and handed it to me. Jane had drawn me lying on the sofa, eyes closed, mouth open.

On Saturday, Father Matt came at his usual time, to find me wearing a gift from Al — new, very baggy jeans that covered my bandage completely. My crutches were in the closet.

Jane and I lounged on the sofa watching morning cartoons. Aunt Cecile sat at the table with Al, drinking coffee.

The men shook hands, greeting each other as old friends. Father Matt then came over to give Jane a new tablet and me a fashion magazine. "How are my girls?" he asked.

"We're fine," I said. "Everybody's fine. Jane wants you to know that she never wets her pants anymore. How about that?"

"Is it true?" Father Matt asked Jane, delighted.

She merely stared at him.

"Where's Adam?" Father Matt said then, looking around.

"I've got him over at my place, doing a few chores," Al said, sitting down at the table again and leaning back in his chair.

Aunt Cecile gaped at him. Obviously she wasn't in on whatever Al was trying to do. Was this the help he'd meant?

He should have let us in on it, I thought, more than a little angry. Replacing the jeans that the nurses had cut short with new, baggy ones to hide the bandage was one thing. I had no idea where he was going with this story about Adam.

"Over at the farm?" Father Matt said. "He'll like that."

"Oh, sure," Al said. "He earns his pay." Then he leaned forward and scowled. "Matt, I've got to tell you what Cecile here probably won't."

My stomach tightened painfully. I saw Aunt Cecile's face go pale.

"What's that?" Matt asked.

"It's that no-good baby sitter you sent up here to watch the kids," Al said. "I ran her off the place awhile back. She was so darned rude to Cecile here, so one day I just up and canned her. I've been keeping an eye on things, and Cecile doesn't need a sitter for these kids. They're good girls, and the boy's over at the farm most of the time anyway. You can look around yourself and see that things are working out."

Father Matt looked around the cabin with an expression of such relief that I nearly cried for him. Sometimes I felt as if I was the adult and he was the child.

"We're fine, Father Matt," I said. "And it's lots nicer without Gerry. She didn't do much of the work, anyway. And Aunt Cecile's a lot better cook."

"You don't mind, Cecile?" Father Matt asked his sister. "This isn't too much for you?"

"Aw, heck, no," Al answered smoothly. "I've been telling her that she won't have enough to do after school starts, so she ought to talk to Bob Sherman — he's on the school board with me — about taking that teaching job at the school."

"Oh, they won't be living here in Monarch River

after the summer," Father Matt said. He looked curiously at Al then. "Didn't Cecile tell you that this was only for the summer?"

"No, I didn't," Aunt Cecile said. She took a sip of her coffee and put her cup down. It rattled in the saucer. "I might stay. I like it here."

She didn't raise her eyes and I knew why. She was panicking again. Al's plan was too complicated to succeed. He should have told me first.

Father Matt stared at his sister. "I don't believe you should make plans like that for yourself without talking to me about it."

Now she looked up. Her eyes were blazing. "I'll do anything I like," she said. "I'm not an invalid."

Father Matt flushed, embarrassed. "I'm sorry, my dear. But all things considered . . ."

I had a lump in my throat that I couldn't swallow.

"Matt," Al said, "I hate to rush you off, especially since you only get to visit once a week, but I did promise these ladies an afternoon riding horses, and we've got to get started pretty soon. I believe it's going to rain again before the day's over."

He guided Father Matt toward the door, barely touching his arm. Father Matt turned back once, thrusting a handful of money at Aunt Cecile.

"Oh, Matt, let me handle it," she said, sounding a bit impatient. "I've got plenty of money."

Father Matt flushed again, said goodbye to all of us, and left. Al shut the door behind him.

170

"I don't want to go horseback riding," I said.

Jane scowled. She didn't like the idea, either.

Al shrugged and laughed. "I wasn't serious. Hey, folks, don't knock what works, okay?"

He left shortly afterward. At the door, Aunt Cecile asked him if he had really seen Adam, or was that only part of the story, too?

"I'm afraid I haven't seen the boy," Al said. "But I think somebody's been coming in the barn at night. Could be him, checking on the dog. He took a fancy to her. If I see him, I'll tell him you're worrying about him."

"Don't turn him in," I blurted.

"Maybe I should," Al said. "He needs a home."

I didn't say anything. Sometimes people who need homes don't get them.

❧ CHAPTER 15 ❧

During the next few days, Al checked on us every afternoon, but he didn't stay long. Each time he spent a
private moment with me, and always he asked the
same question.

"How is it really? No bull, little lady."

And always I was able to say truthfully, "It's okay.
Really. No bull."

One hot, bright day, he took me back to the hospital to have the stitches removed from my leg, and
nodded approvingly when I didn't so much as
squeak. "Good girl," he said.

On the way home, he stopped by his farm so that I
could see Goldie. She still lived in the barn with her
pup, Silver, and I was certain that she recognized me,
although she looked terribly anxious because I was
standing so close.

"Goldie's just now starting to trust me," Al said.
"I don't worry her by touching her baby, though.

Pretty soon she'll learn that nobody here will hurt her."

"I wish Jane could learn that," I said.

"Maybe all that happened to Goldie was being tossed out when she wasn't cute enough anymore, or too much trouble to feed. I think more happened to Jane than being abandoned, so she's got more to come to peace with."

There was a box of dog treats on a shelf near Goldie, and I took one out and tossed it to her. Her tail flapped twice before she reached for it.

"I didn't buy those treats," Al said. "Found 'em here one morning. I expect that Goldie's visitor left the box behind by mistake."

"You think it was Adam, right?" I said. "But I can't imagine him buying anything for anybody."

"A dog's safe," Al said. "You can afford to be nice to a dog when you can't bear risking it with anybody else."

"Maybe you could leave Adam a note," I said. "Tell him he could come home if he wanted. Let him know that Aunt Cecile and Jane and I will be here for the rest of the summer."

"You think that's what he wants to hear?" Al asked.

I shrugged. "No, probably not. But I know that he knocked out Snyder's windows because of how the man treated Aunt Cecile. He likes her, even if he hates

Jane and me. Maybe he'd like to live out the summer with her, if he knew."

"Maybe," Al said.

I tossed Goldie another treat. "Of course, Snyder's still in the summer camp. If Adam came back now, he'd probably get in trouble."

"Maybe he's keeping watch over things, to see how long this Snyder hangs around," Al said.

I looked up at him. "You think so?"

"It's how I would handle it myself," Al said. "Adam didn't strike me as stupid."

"Ha," I said. "He is, though."

Al didn't reply, and we didn't talk about Adam again. When we got home, Aunt Cecile served us strawberry shortcake out on the porch, and Jane, scowling, presented me with a picture. It showed me standing beside a tall man, and both of us were smiling. A dark cloud hung over our heads.

"You're mad because you were left behind?" I asked.

Her lower lip stuck out.

"Sorry," I said. "I thought you didn't like Al."

She took her bowl of strawberry shortcake inside the cabin and ate alone at the table. Al had a terrible time not laughing. So did I.

Father Matt's next two visits went very well. Al was there each time, but Father Matt didn't seem to mind.

After the second visit I told Al that I didn't think he needed to hang around so much anymore.

"Aunt Cecile's getting along pretty good now," I told him. "She's even using her left arm for some things, and she hardly ever has trouble with words. Sometimes she forgets things, but not as bad as before."

"I forget things," Al said. "All the time. That means that you've got a lot of things to think about. But if it's all right, boss lady, I do believe I'll drop in the way I have been. Just in case. Anyway, I've got a surprise ordered up for Monday, so you can bet I'll be here to see what happens."

He wouldn't give me a clue about the surprise, but only ordered me not to hint to Aunt Cecile that anything was going on.

On Monday, while we were putting away the breakfast dishes, Al showed up with a young man in a gray uniform.

"Cecile, today's the day the phone gets put in," Al said.

She stared at him. "I don't want a phone," she said. "One of the charms about this place is not having a phone."

"This is for the girls," Al said, "not for you. Mary Jack's clumsy with tools, so who knows what she'll do to herself next. And any day now Jane's going to start talking up a storm. When the time comes, she'll need a phone, the way young folks do."

I expected Aunt Cecile to argue, but she didn't. Al and the man in the uniform disappeared for a while, and then we heard the sounds of machinery. I ran out to see what was going on.

A peculiar, heavy-wheeled truck was inching down the path from the road, crushing ferns and splintering twigs. From it a long contraption stuck up into the air, ending with a basket. A man in a hard hat stood in the basket, stringing wire along the power poles that brought electricity from the road to the cabin.

This was too interesting for Jane to miss. I brought her out from the cabin, and together we watched the men bring the line all the way to the roof. Before the day was over, a bright red telephone sat on the kitchen counter.

"Now," Al said to Aunt Cecile, "who are you going to call first?"

She called Father Matt, but got Jill instead. That was a conversation I didn't want to overhear, so I strolled out on the porch with Jane. Al followed, grinning.

"Your aunt took it pretty good, didn't she?" he said.

"Yeah," I said. My mind was busy with something. "Do you think she'll really stay here when summer is over?"

"It would be good for her. And we need her."

"To teach in the school? But she isn't well yet." I couldn't believe how much he was taking for granted.

"There's a good six weeks at least before school starts," he said. "Look how much better she is now than the first time I showed up here."

Aunt Cecile came out on the porch, interrupting our conversation.

"So how was it, talking on the phone?" Al asked, grinning.

Aunt Cecile didn't smile back. "Honestly, that woman is such a stupid . . ."

I cringed. She wasn't going to use *that* word again, was she?

"Neurotic," Aunt Cecile finished.

I let out the breath I'd been holding.

"What's the problem?" Al asked.

I glanced at her, in time to see her exchange a meaningful look with Al.

The problem was us — Jane and me.

"That's okay," I said. "I know she doesn't want me back. But what about Jane?"

"My brother will take care of you," Aunt Cecile said. "Don't worry about anything. He won't put up with her silly behavior much longer. They'll end up going separate ways."

She didn't know the first thing about the foster care system. If Father Matt and his wife got a divorce, there was no way the social workers would leave Jane and me with him.

And there was the problem of Adam, too. Nobody but us knew he was missing.

I couldn't stand hearing more. "I'm going to take Jane for a walk to the pond," I said, and I left them on the porch together.

Jane and I were resting on the side of the pond opposite from the path when Al passed on his way out to his truck. He shouted a cheerful goodbye to us and we waved back.

Jane, on her stomach, watched fish in the pond. Their speckled brown bodies were almost invisible as they slid through the dark water. After a few minutes, she sat up and began drawing.

Aunt Cecile called to me from the other side of the pond. I walked around to see what she wanted.

"You're worried about being put in another foster home," she said. "I don't blame you. But were you all that happy with Jill? She's so exasperating. Not motherly at all."

I shrugged. "I was managing. I'm just sorry that I let her down."

Aunt Cecile slipped her arm around my shoulders. "You didn't let her down. She let you down."

"It doesn't make any difference which way it was," I said. "I have to move again. But it's all right for me. I can handle it. It's Jane. They'll put her in an institution."

My throat thickened and I couldn't talk any longer. Aunt Cecile squeezed me and said, "Let me think about it. Maybe I can figure something out. I only wish we knew where Adam was."

We circled the pond and sat down near where Jane was busy drawing. Her face was bent over her tablet, and her fine, pale hair stood out around her head, seeming almost to glow against the dark woods behind her.

"Heavens," Aunt Cecile said. "You know what she reminds me of? A black-eyed Susan."

I knew what she meant. The daisies grew wild along the path, and Jane did look like them, with her light hair like petals around her face with its dark, velvety eyes.

Jane tore off one page and began another. A duck skidded along the pond, leaving a wake. Somewhere a crow screamed and another chattered an answer.

"I love this place," Aunt Cecile said. "I want to stay here. I'll have an electric furnace put in and bring up some of my things from my apartment. Al said he knows a good carpenter who could add on a larger bedroom, maybe a nice bathroom, and a laundry room. And I'll buy a dryer! How about that, Mary Jack? No more clotheslines."

It would be nice. It would be wonderful.

Jane brought us her newest picture and gave it to me to see first. She had drawn a black-eyed Susan. I'd had no idea that she was listening to us.

"Nice," I said. "See, Aunt Cecile? She's drawn a daisy."

Jane's face broke into a wide smile. *A smile!*

"My God," Aunt Cecile said. "I wonder if her name is Daisy!"

Jane's smile grew even wider.

"She knows that black-eyed Susans are daisies because you told us the names of all the flowers when we came here," I said, unable to believe that Jane had told us her real name.

"That was way back in May!" Aunt Cecile said. "The black-eyed Susans weren't in bloom then." She swung to look at me. "How did *you* know what they were called?"

"They grew in the yard at my last foster home," I said.

Jane — or Daisy, if that was her name — took the drawing back and marched to her crayons. She sat down to draw again.

"I suppose she could have learned what they were called somewhere else, too," Aunt Cecile said. "But why that ecstatic smile?"

I got goose bumps remembering the smile. What if Aunt Cecile was right?

Jane was back. She had added two figures to her picture, one representing Aunt Cecile and one representing me. And now the daisy was wearing blue pants, like Jane's.

I pointed to the daisy. "Is this you?"

Jane smiled.

"Maybe her name is Susan," I said to Aunt Cecile, half sick from uncertainty. "Are you Susan?" I asked Jane.

"Daisy," she said, her voice husky and quiet. And then she smiled again.

Aunt Cecile burst into tears, and so did I. And then so did Jane.

"Jeez," Adam said from behind us. "I can't stand it when women bawl."

We leaped up and shouted his name. We would have hugged him, but I think that Aunt Cecile knew as well as I that it would have sent him back to wherever he'd been hiding.

"Where have you been?" Aunt Cecile cried.

Adam shrugged in the exasperating way he had and said, "Around. Hey, Don Snyder's gone. Different people are in the cabin now. They got here this morning."

"So it's safe for you to come back," I said. "Did Al leave you a note?"

Another shrug. "Yeah. I left the dog biscuits behind, so he knew I'd been visiting Goldie and Silver. She's looking good now. Have you seen her?"

I nodded.

He grinned, a rare expression. "She does tricks. She'll fetch a stick and roll over. But she jumps up on me too much. I like it, but maybe that's why her owners got rid of her."

"She lets you touch her?" I exclaimed.

He stared at me, the old, hostile stare. "Of course. We're pals."

I ground my teeth with jealousy.

"You're coming back, aren't you?" Aunt Cecile said. "Your clothes could do with a washing, and you don't look as though you've been eating very well."

I wouldn't have started out by nagging him, but to my surprise, Adam didn't get mad at her. "I might," he said. "For the rest of the summer. If you're staying, that is."

We filled him in on the developments. When Aunt Cecile told him about my accident with the axe, he looked at me with such disgust that I wanted to double up my fist and knock him into the pond.

"Well, it wouldn't have happened if you'd stayed here!" I shouted.

"It wouldn't have happened if you were half as smart as you think you are," he retaliated.

"Oh, hush up, both of you," Aunt Cecile said.

We did, and in the silence, Jane — or Daisy — said, "Hi."

Adam gaped and I laughed.

"Jeez," he said. "She talks. I don't think I can stand it."

We celebrated that night, with steak and baked potatoes, and a platter of fresh fruit, and hot French bread. Al provided the steak, because Aunt Cecile phoned him from the cabin to tell him about Adam and Daisy, and he invited himself to dinner.

It was the best night of all my life.

Afterward, when Al went home, and Adam had built a fire, and Jane — I mean Daisy — had her bath, the four of us sat in the main room and watched television together. We were an absolutely perfect family.

Daisy gave us another picture before we went to bed. She showed all of us standing in front of chairs and sofas — she still had a terrible time drawing people who were sitting — and we were all smiling. This time she'd drawn herself as a small, thin girl with light yellow hair.

"This is you?" I said.

"Daisy," she said.

Aunt Cecile nodded. "Daisy," she said. "We won't forget." She tacked the drawing to the wall over the mantel where we could all enjoy it.

"I believe we could make it here over the winter," she said, looking around at us. "With a furnace and a dryer, and another bedroom . . ."

"We should have separate bedrooms," I said eagerly, without considering that maybe she didn't mean what I thought she meant.

"Okay, two bedrooms, and a better bath." She eyed Adam thoughtfully. "And one car, to which only I will have keys."

"Oh, cripes," Adam said. "I can drive!"

I bit my lip so I wouldn't cry. "Come on, Ja . . . , I mean Daisy. Time for bed."

"No," Daisy said.

"I knew it!" Adam exclaimed behind me as I dragged Daisy down the hall. "I knew that if she learned to talk, there'd be trouble."

I tucked my sister in, listening to the others making plans down the hall. Some of their ideas might not work out, but others might. One way or another, even *we* could work out.

Outside the river rushed between the rocks, and wind sang in the eaves, and everything was just as it had been for more years than anyone here could remember. We weren't so unusual, I thought — just one more family living in the cabin beyond the end of the road. I was safe, and I could fall asleep without biting my nails. And someday, maybe, we'd tell Father Matt what really happened.

"Good night, Mary Jack," Daisy said hoarsely.

"Good night, Daisy."